Eric Br

A special signed edition, limited to
350 numbered copies.
This is number:

40

Starship Fall

Starship Fall

Eric Brown

With an introduction by
Tony Ballantyne

NewCon Press
England

First edition, published in the UK April 2009
by NewCon Press
41 Wheatsheaf Road, Alconbury Weston, Cambs, PE28 4LF

NCP 013 (signed hardback)
NCP 014 (signed softback)

10 9 8 7 6 5 4 3 2 1

ISBN:

978-1-907069-02-4 (hardback)
978-1-900679-03-1 (softback)

Cover illustration by Dominic Harman
Cover layout and design by Andy Bigwood

Book layout by Storm Constantine

Printed in the UK by the MPG Book Group

Starship Fall is dedicated to
Michael and Ivy Tian Xuesong Greenwood

Starship Fall: An Introduction

By Tony Ballantyne

"There is always something strikingly probable about the futures that Eric Brown writes... No matter how dark the future that Eric Brown imagines, the hope of redemption is always present. No matter how alien the world he describes, there is always something hauntingly familiar about the situations that unfold there."

I wrote the above 5 years ago, for the introduction to the Spanish version of New York Nights, and I was reminded of it when I found it amongst the quotes at the front of Eric Brown's hugely successful novel, *Helix*. This novella is a very different piece of work, but the idea still holds true.

Although a stand alone story which can easily be read as such, Starship Fall also provides the sequel to Eric's Starship Summer, a delightful novella set on the world of Chalcedony which deals with a group of broken people helping each other to put their lives back together.

Now, SF is a broad church; it is a field well served with battling robots, Artificial Intelligences, cyber detectives and expletive ridden tales of torture written in the first person present tense. All this shows the genre is healthy and avoiding stagnation, or at least is mistaken by some for that fact

But there is also a place within it for tales of warmth and reflection and friendship. This is one such book. It is harder to write this sort of thing than you would imagine, and it is all the more welcome for the breadth it gives to the field.

Eric has been writing for over thirty years now, and does it so well that it is easy to miss what he does. His books are easy to read, they portray sympathetic, recognisable characters drawn from real life, and they are effectively plotted. Anyone too exposed to the overwritten prose that excuses itself as cutting edge literature may think the preceding paragraph mildly insulting to Eric's work, but they would be missing the point.

The advice given time and again to those wanting to be writers is to ensure that you don't place anything in the reader's way to remind them that they are reading a book. Establishing character, building a plot, explaining motive without resorting to simply telling the reader what is going on: these are skills that every writer must get to grips with.

To do all this when you can't even rely on the reader having a familiarity with the everyday world around them is what makes SF so difficult to write. Or I should say, so difficult to write well. Eric Brown is so highly regarded amongst his peers because they recognise just how good he is at what he does. He could write a convincing story about a pair of carpet slippers, comfortable and familiar, but, just as in this story, he would still grip the reader with tension as the story built to a climax.

Eric has recently moved to a tiny thatched cottage in Cambridgeshire. He lives there with his Medievalist wife and young daughter, cooking delicious curries and gradually renovating the property. Experience suggests that when he has made the place comfortable, unpacked his large library of SF books and got the guest accommodation sorted he will probably move again, though he fervently denies this.

Eric is a prolific writer with a wide back catalogue, he is a voracious and knowledgeable reader. He reviews SF for the Guardian in between writing short stories and novellas. He is currently working on Cosmopath, the third volume of the Bengal Station trilogy, and a series of stories featuring the captain of a salvage starship, set in the year 2300.

If this is your first taste of Eric Brown's work, welcome to his world!

Otherwise, welcome back!

Enjoy!

One

I lead a quiet life here in Magenta Bay, on Chalcedony, Delta Pavonis IV; some might even call my existence boring. I read a lot, and walk, and swim in the bay, and sometimes I drive into the mountains to admire the fine views along the coast. Three or four nights a week – the highlights of my life, as far as I'm concerned – I meet my friends in the Fighting Jackeral; occasionally they come round to my place, the old starship situated on the headland north of the bay, or I visit them, and we while away the evening with a meal and drinks and conversation. My friends are Matt Sommers, the famous crystal artist; his partner Maddie Chamberlain, a wonderful Englishwoman who loves Matt to bits; Hawk, the piratical space pilot and his alien girlfriend, the fey and elusive Kee. They are more than friends to me now, five years after my arrival on the planet; they are family, and I love them all.

* * *

Autumn comes late to this latitude of Chalcedony, immediately after the tempestuous storm season, and it's a wonderful period of long warm days – a slow sliding into winter which is never really cold up here. Autumn is perhaps my favourite time of year, when the tourist season is winding down, and the concessions along the front close up for another six months and the locals, after the work of summer, kick back and relax and enjoy their hard won gains. The silver shola trees become golden and the Ring of Tharssos, that girdle of shattered moonlets which encircles the planet, turns molten in the long hours of sunset.

I was looking forward to a few months of doing nothing, of reading the classics – I still prefer real books to the screens you can get these days: call me old-fashioned, if you like – of walking in the mountains and seeing my friends. Nothing much had happened in Magenta Bay for five years, and for all I knew nothing else would happen for another five. Not that I would be complaining.

That morning I woke at seven, as usual, then showered and went for a walk along the beach, around the bay and back again. I breakfasted on the balcony of my starship, the *Mantis*, looking out across the mirror-calm surface of the bay, watching the play of sunlight on the water, like restless sequins, and the dark shadows of the jackeral shoals as they came in from the ocean in search of food.

I was on my second coffee when I noticed the woman, and I wondered why I had failed to see her earlier. She was lying on the sands below the nose of the *Mantis*, so that only her long tanned legs showed. Curious – Matt claims that I wanted to ascertain whether or not the rest of this Venus matched what I had seen so far – I stood and looked down at the reclining beauty.

I'd assumed that she was sun-bathing – though why she might be doing so at eight in the morning I was at a loss to guess. But one look was enough to tell me that she was doing nothing of the kind. She wore a black evening dress, for one thing, and her head was twisted so that she stared back along the beach towards the township.

I hurried from the *Mantis*, wallowed through the fine red drifts of sand, and knelt before the stricken woman.

I realised that she was older than I had first thought; and though she possessed a striking beauty, it was not that vital pearlescent lustre of early womanhood but the more weathered glamour of early middle-age: I guessed she was in her mid-forties.

She was dusky and raven haired, and her mouth was a red slash that seemed almost, *almost*, too wide for her thin face so that at first it seemed disproportionate.

I judged that she was not asleep but unconscious, and reached out to take her pulse. Her tanned wrist was thin, but the pulse seemed healthy enough. I sat on my haunches, wondering what the hell to do, and took in this unexpected and beauteous jetsam.

Only then did I notice the smell; it was the scent of smoke, a certain type of smoke I had never encountered before. It emanated from her flesh, and as I inhaled and wondered who she was and what she was doing here, the woman opened her eyes and stared at me.

Her eyes were mahogany brown, and their light sent the shadows beneath them into stark relief; so that my first impression of her, conscious, was that she was ill.

"Of course, it's wholly unfair; I was scaling the heights. And then *that* came along, and where was I then? I was good, *great*, but I could never compete with... with *that*."

It came out in a rush, as if confided to a life-long intimate, and I was open-mouthed and quite at a loss to know what to say.

Then her eyes refocused suddenly, and she snapped, "And who might you be, if I might ask?"

"David," I stammered. "David Conway..." I gestured back to the *Mantis*. "I live there."

She sat up, wincing, a graceful hand bracing the small of her exquisite back. "Well, Conway, why don't you make yourself useful and help me back to my place?"

I stood and reached out, not quite knowing where to touch her, for all the world like some flustered flunky at her beck and call. I grabbed her elbow and eased her upright. Perpendicular now, she stood a good few inches taller than me; her breasts fell a little and filled the material of her dress, and I was made more aware of her curves. (Maddie playfully accused me of sexism when I recounted this, but I set this down as an accurate account of my response to the woman. Recall, I had been alone and celibate for more than five years at the time.)

"Well, don't just stand there gaping at me, Conway." She pointed to a large villa a couple of hundred metres away around the curve of the bay. "Help me home, if you would be so kind."

I slipped my arm around her waist; she leaned into me and I struggled with her through the shifting sands. Ten minutes later – she walked like a zombie on valium – we made it to the verandah of her expensive domicile and I eased her up the steps.

She opened a sliding glass door, shrugged me off and staggered inside. I had a glimpse of a dark lounge hung, I thought, with works of art. At the far end of the room, in the shadows, I made out a beautiful, dark-haired girl, and her similarity to the older woman made me assume it was her daughter.

"You don't make a habit of sunbathing this early, do you?"

My words halted her progress into the room. She turned, and the look in her eyes could be described as venomous. "Don't be so bloody ridiculous, Conway."

I backed off and raised my hands in surrender.

She glared at me, then said, "You don't have the slightest idea who I am, do you?"

I opened my mouth, doing a fair imitation of a landed jackeral.

Before I could agree that she was indeed correct, she said, "Of course you bloody well don't!" and pressed a panel on the wall beside the door which swished a pair of curtains across the plate glass. The show was over, folks.

Smiling to myself, and wondering exactly who the hell she might be, I made my way home.

Two

"You mean to tell me, David," Maddie said, leaning forward incredulously, "that you hadn't heard *she* had moved to Magenta Bay?"

It was late afternoon, and I'd slipped into the Fighting Jackeral for a beer to find Maddie ensconced in a lounger on the verandah, a fruit juice before her on the table. Matt was beside her, contemplating his ice cold beer as a man might a pot of gold.

Maddie stared at me and said, "No, seriously; I mean, you *hadn't* heard?"

Matt winked at me and said, "Maddie, the poor man obviously hadn't. She only moved here a few days ago, after all. Leave him be or tell him, or something."

I smiled. "Obviously I don't get out enough. Go on, who is she?"

Maddie sat upright and announced, "Only Carlotta Chakravorti-Luna, is who."

I blinked. "Sorry, none the wiser. An artist?"

"You are a sad specimen, David Conway," Maddie said.

Matt came to my defence. "To be honest, David, I only heard of her last week when Maddie said she was moving here."

Maddie leaned forward. "And you've actually met her, David. Lucky you! What was she like?"

"Lucky me? I don't think so. She was positively... Well, I don't know how to describe her. Arrogant, dismissive – and probably drunk and drugged, or both."

"Tell me again exactly what happened?" Maddie asked like a sensation-seeking teenager.

So I recounted the meeting again, this time describing the little I'd seen in the woman's lounge.

"Apparently she has a holo-deck playing all the time," Maddie said. "She's obsessed. The gossip writers say it's pathological."

"I don't understand—" I began.

"Luna is — was — a big holo star on Earth, back at the turn of the century. She's the daughter of the famous Indian director, Ramesh Chakravorti, and the Italian actress Gina Luna—" Maddie stopped suddenly and stared at someone standing behind me.

I turned.

Carlotta Chakravorti-Luna stood over me, appearing at least seven feet tall from my seated perspective. She looked stunning in a scarlet dress, with midnight hair falling over one eye. She had a hand lodged on one hip and her bearing was imperious.

If she'd heard Maddie, she had the grace not to let on. Instead she nodded to Maddie and Matt, then looked at me. "Conway, I do think I owe you an apology. The way I behaved this morning was *way* beyond decency, and I owe you not only an apology, but an explanation. If you are free some time…?" She let it hang.

I spluttered something like a callow juvenile.

"Come round to the villa one evening, for drinks. Would tomorrow suit? Eight, say?"

And with another nod at Matt and Maddie, Carlotta Chakravorti-Luna swept from the verandah, sashayed through the main bar of the Jackeral and exited at the front.

Maddie was watching me, eyes the size of moons, her jaw halfway to her knees. Matt merely leaned over, jabbed me playfully in the ribs, and winked.

I sat back, wondering how I felt about the summons to the villa of a once famous but still ravishing holo star.

"So… tell me more about Carla Chakrawhatever-Lunacy," I said.

Three

The next day, I strolled around the bay to Matt and Maddie's place. They lived on the southern headland opposite mine, in a two-storey beachfront dome backed by pines. Last night, before last orders, Matt had invited me over to take a look at what he was working on. It was mid-afternoon and hot when I arrived. Maddie was sitting on the verandah overlooking the bay, reading a novel I had loaned her.

She looked up and shaded her eyes when I climbed the steps. "And might the footsore traveller be in need of a beer, by any chance?"

"You're a mind-reader, Maddie."

She fetched me an ice cold bottle from the cooler and escorted me through the dome to Matt's studio.

"Isn't it tonight you have the assignation with Magenta's biggest celebrity?" Maddie asked with a sly smile.

"Hardly an assignation, Maddie."

"I'm not so sure. If you want my opinion, I think she has the hots for you."

I laughed. "Come on! Is that likely?" I think I coloured as she grinned at me.

"I don't know. You're quite a catch, David. Lean, fit, personable. And famous, in your own right."

I snorted. "And you know what I think about fame," I said.

We came to the studio, a light-filled space on the dome's ground-floor. Matt was wearing only a pair of baggy shorts, his preferred attire when working. He stood over a computer keypad and played it like a musician.

He looked up when we entered and nodded at my beer. "Good idea, sir." He moved to a cooler in the corner of the room. "Maddie?"

"I don't want to feel left out," she said. "How's it coming on?"

Matt passed her a beer and we sat on folding chairs in the middle of the studio. I looked around. Other than stacked crystal boards, old canvases and the odd unfinished sculpture, there was nothing on show to indicate his latest project.

"Almost finished, and I think it's okay. Should be ready in a few days." He looked at me. "I'm having a private viewing here in a couple of weeks, if you'd like to come along."

"Try keeping me away," I said. "What are you working on?" He was notoriously reticent about work-in-progress, as if to talk about his work might dissipate the creative impetus.

"Seeing as how it's almost done..." He leaned over and tapped a few keys on the com-pad. "I wanted to get away from what I've doing lately – the emotion crystals. I felt I'd done enough in that medium for the time being. I was getting stale–"

"That's not what that New York critic said about your last exhibition," Maddie put in.

Matt snorted. "What do critics know? Anyway, I thought I'd try something completely different."

In the air at the far end of the dome, I saw two figures materialise. They were naked, though abstract; that is, it was impossible to identify the man and woman: they stood as representative, perhaps, of the human race.

"We live in a cynical age, David. Perhaps we always have. In the past, my art has been an attempt to counter that cynicism. After all, nihilism's an easy get out – it's far harder to be constructively positive about the human condition, but I try."

As I watched, the figures reached out towards each other, came together and merged; they became one, and then something odd happened. They seemed to explode into a million shards of light, which hung in a nimbus and slowly expanded to fill the far end of the dome in a scintillating sphere.

"I wanted to say something about what I have with Maddie," Matt explained. "I wanted somehow to capture and encapsulate the feeling we call love."

"It's... beautiful," I said.

"It's not just visual." Matt smiled and gestured. "Go ahead, walk into it."

I looked at him questioningly, but he just urged me on. Beside him, Maddie nursed her beer and smiled.

I did as instructed, left my seat and strode towards the radiant globe. I paused before it, wondering what species of art this might be, and what I might experience when I stepped into the light.

I took a breath and advanced.

How to describe the sensations that overtook me then? I was bombarded with emotions – the experience was akin to Matt's crystals, though much more powerful. It was as if I had taken a drug which allowed me to access all the euphoria, all the love, I had ever felt for everyone throughout my life. I moved around in the light like a sleepwalker, my head filled with the joyous wonder of life and love...

Then I passed through the other side of the globe, and instead of coming crashing back down to mundane reality, the upbeat feelings of unity and positivism remained with me.

I walked around the sphere, marvelling, and returned to where Matt and Maddie were sitting, watching me closely.

"Well?" Matt said.

I shook my head, still in a daze. "How the hell did you do it, Matt?"

He smiled. "Trade secret, David. It's not too different in principle to my crystals, though I employ nano-tech instead of alien stones."

"It's remarkable. It'll be a hit." I smiled at my friends, as they sat side by side and held hands, and I think a part of me envied them the love that had gone into Matt's creating this, his latest masterpiece.

"There'll be about a dozen spheres when I've finished," he went on, "all representative of different kinds of love. I'm still tweaking two or three of them."

"I can't wait for the private viewing," I said.

Maddie's com bleeped, and she stood and moved away to answer the call.

"Well," Matt said, "I'm delighted you liked it."

"Liked?" I said. "I loved it!"

Matt laughed, and looked across at Maddie. He frowned. Maddie was speaking hurriedly into her com, looking worried.

She cut the connection and hurried over to us. She looked from Matt to me, her face white.

"That was Hawk," she said.

My heart jumped. "What?" I said.

"He asked if we could come over. It's Kee. He said she's disappeared, and he fears for her safety."

* * *

We climbed aboard Matt's ground-effect vehicle and tore off down the coast to Hawk's starship junkyard three kays out of Magenta.

"What do you mean, Kee's vanished and he fears for her safety?" I asked, leaning forward between the front seats as I tried to make sense of Hawk's communiqué.

Maddie bit her lip. "That was all he said. Kee's gone. And he was afraid something might have happened to her. He said come over, then cut the connection."

She looked at her wrist-com, stabbed Hawk's code, and shook her head. "He's not answering, damn it."

Five minutes later we turned and hovered through the

archway bearing the legend: HAWKSWORTH & CO. constructed from scrap metal. Hawk's place never failed to stir in me a heady rush of emotion. I was transported back in time to my youth in Canada, when I spent long weekends staring through the perimeter fence at the starships landing and taking off from Vancouver spaceport.

Hawk's yard was filled with reminders of my childhood, starfaring vessels from the dozen Lines that went out of business thirty years ago with the advent of the Telemass process, ships as small as two-person exploration vessels right up to bulky, lumbering cargo vessels; they bore the livery of their respective owners, faded now with the years.

Hawk was waiting for us on the balcony of the starship which doubled as his office and living quarters. He was leaning against the rail, looking down, a beer gripped in his right fist.

We jumped from the car and hurried up the steps.

Hawk is a big man, six-five, and broad across the shoulders. His pilot's augmentations add to his stature: the cerebral implant spans his shoulders like a yoke, and the spinal jacks he had fitted a few years ago give him a severe, ramrod posture.

I would have said that he was the happiest person I knew, leaving aside the love-birds Matt and Maddie. He had a wonderful if odd woman in Kee, a member of the native alien Ashentay race, and a couple of times a year he took a starship full of tourists through the portal of the Yall's golden column on a jaunt across the galaxy.

But he was not the world's happiest man today.

"What the hell's going on, Hawk?" I said as we reached the balcony.

He glared at his beer, and something in his eyes indicated that it was not his first of the day.

Maddie embraced him. "Kee...?" she whispered.

He gestured with his bottle to the ship's entrance behind him. "Help yourself to beers," he said.

Matt said, "This is hardly the time to drink – what's happening?"

Hawk pushed himself away from the rail and strode into the ship. "Come in."

We followed him through the cramped coms-room he used as an office and into the lounge, an amphitheatre that had once been the ship's bridge. The sunken sofas were strewn with clothing – Kee's flimsy wraps and leggings.

Hawk strode around the lounge to the sliding doors and walked onto the long balcony which overlooked the yard. He indicated a table on the balcony.

There was a note on the table, covered with large, childish hand-writing. Maddie picked it up, looking to Hawk for permission to read it. He nodded.

"*I'm sorry, Hawk,*" she read aloud. "*Time, now. Inland for rites. Couldn't tell you. Secret. I hope I will see you again. Kee.*"

At this last sentence, Hawk turned a stricken gaze on us. "She's been acting oddly for weeks, quiet, uncommunicative. I shrugged it off as Kee, as alien. She gets like that from time to time. Christ knows, it's hard enough having a relationship with a human woman–"

"Tell me about it," Matt quipped, earning an elbow in the ribs from Maddie.

"But Kee's alien, and they do things differently."

"Hawk," I said gently. "You said you feared for her safety...?"

He took a deep breath and nodded. "In the early days, when we first got together... I wanted to know more about her, her people. I reckoned if I knew more about the Ashentay, then... I don't know... then maybe it'd be easier to understand Kee, to work out how best to respond to her. I knew I was in love, whatever that means, and I wanted to keep her, so I quizzed her about her people, their rites and customs."

He stopped there. Matt prompted, "And?"

"And I remember she once told me about a certain rite that each Ashentay has to undergo around the age of thirty. It's one of the many they take part in throughout their lives."

Maddie said in a small voice, "And how old is Kee, Hawk?"

He said, "Thirty."

"And this rite?" Matt asked.

Hawk nodded. "It's called smoking the bones."

"Sounds... exactly like something the Ashentay would cook up," I said. They were a strange race, with beliefs that made little sense to human observers.

"What does it consist of?" Maddie asked.

"The Ashentay are a hunter-gatherer people," Hawk said. "They have been for hundreds of thousands of years. They hunt a certain animal... I forget what they call it. Anyway, they don't hunt this beast for meat – it's inedible, apparently – but for its bones."

Matt echoed, "For its bones?"

"They kill the animal, strip it to its skeleton, dry its bones and smoke them. I don't know whether they grind the bones to dust, or actually smoke the bones like pipes, but anyway, they smoke its bones and go into a trance. While in this trance, this altered state, Kee told me they're granted a foretaste of the future, of their individual destinies."

I said, "And Kee's gone to take part in this ceremony?"

"I put two and two together: the Ashentay smoke the bones in their thirtieth year, at a sacred location inland of here: and in the note Kee said... she said she hoped she would see me again."

Maddie shook her head. "But why shouldn't she?"

Hawk hesitated, then said, "The effect of smoking its bones is sometimes lethal. Kee said that the fatality rate is often thirty per cent. And this is accepted by the fatalistic Ashentay as their destiny..."

I almost said something bigoted about primitive belief systems, but restrained myself.

Maddie reached out and took Hawk's hand. Matt said, "Then there's only one thing for it, Hawk, we've got to either try to stop her before she smokes the stuff... or be on hand afterwards to help her."

Hawk looked bleak. He nodded. "I've been away almost a week, down past MacIntyre delivering a starship habitat to a rich industrialist. I don't know when Kee set off."

"Do you know where the sacred site is, Hawk?"

He nodded. "She's mentioned it in the past. It's in the central massifs, high up beyond a native village called Dar, about a hundred kilometres from here."

"And was she on foot?" Maddie asked.

"That's just it, I don't know. She can drive, but rarely does. I checked, and she hasn't hired a car locally. But she might have gone into MacIntyre and hired one there."

Matt nodded and looked out across the junkyard. On the horizon, the bloated, blood-red orb of Delta Pavonis was lowering itself slowly into the ocean.

"It'll be dark in an hour," he said. "We'd never make it through the mountain pass. How about we get some provisions together, camping gear and food, and set off first thing in the morning?"

Hawk said, "I don't know how Kee might take what she'd see as our interference... but we've got to try to find her."

"That's settled, then," Maddie said. "Right, we're going back to the Jackeral for a meal, Hawk. Come with us, and I won't take no for an answer."

Hawk smiled, knowing better than to argue with Maddie. "That sounds like a civilised idea."

As we climbed down from the ship and approached Matt's ground-effect vehicle, Maddie said, "But David won't be joining us, will you David?" She looked at me archly.

Hawk glanced my way. I'd forgotten all about my invitation for drinks from the one-time famous holo star, and I wasn't sure

I wanted to be reminded.

Maddie went on, "He has an *assignation*, don't you, David? With a beautiful holo star."

She regaled Hawk with the story as we drove back to Magenta Bay.

Hawk said, "That's odd. I once knew her lover, the pilot Ed Grainger... I wonder what brought her here?"

"Maybe the same as what brought all of us here," I said. "Maybe she's fleeing the demons of her past."

Maddie laughed. "Well, we'll be relying on you to find out, David."

Four

On the stroke of eight I rapped on the glass door and stood back, clearing my throat nervously.

The door swished open and the ex-holo star beamed at me. "Conway, how nice of you to come. And you've brought something; how sweet. Do come in."

I passed her the bottle of Chardonnay and stepped into the lounge; the lighting was low and so was the music, something classical and... dare I say it... intimate?

I managed to drag my eyes away from Carlotta; she was not so much dressed as wrapped. In fact, sprayed on might be a better word to describe her *faux* chamois costume, a scant spiral of flesh-toned material which wound round her breasts, crossed her flat stomach and by some miracle managed to conceal her crotch. She was holding a long-stemmed champagne glass, and by the abstracted glaze in her eyes I guessed she'd been drinking for quite a while.

She swayed across to a bar and deposited the wine.

I looked around the long lounge. The first thing I noticed, much to my relief, was that we were not alone. Three guests stood chatting at the far end of the room, and standing beside them was the young woman I had yesterday assumed was Carlotta's daughter. I wondered at the rivalry that might exist between the two women, for the younger was as beautiful, if not more so, than the older.

"Can I get you something, Conway?"

"Ah... a beer would be nice."

While she poured an ice cold wheat beer, I looked around at

the artwork on the walls. They were, I saw, stills taken from various holo-movies; it was half a minute before I realised that the women depicted were all Carlotta, in a dozen or so very different roles.

"I see you're admiring the shots," she said, passing my glass. "They're the work of Ed Kalcheck, and needless to say they're all originals."

"Kalcheck?" I asked.

"The holo-movie director, of course. He directed most of my movies, and occasionally selected shots which he felt worked on their own merit. My favourite is this one," she went on, indicating the shot of herself against the backdrop of a harbour, the full moon lighting her face. "It's from the award-winning Charisma, of course, where I played a telepathic double-agent. I thought it my finest performance. You must know it – the telepath is tortured by the subjective truth she divines in the human soul. Her decision to turn against her former pay-masters symbolises her despair at ever learning what she craves: objective truth."

"Ah..." I said, colouring. "Yes; yes. A great film."

She swept on, "And of course you must recognise this one..." indicating a woman whose expression seems torn by anguish. "It's from Winter's Children, where I played a woman with the ability to look into the future, at the tragedy that awaits her."

"Of course," I said. "A classic."

"I thought so too, Conway."

She led me around the room, giving me not only a potted filmography of everything she'd ever appeared in, but a good indication of her personality. I wondered if breathtaking beauty was always accompanied by a monstrous ego.

I glanced over at the other guests; they were chatting away as if oblivious of our presence. I recognised none of them as locals, and wondered if they, like Luna, were off-worlders.

"But I'm not the only celebrity here tonight, Conway," she laughed brightly with, I thought, a stab at false modesty.

"Oh..." I looked across at the guests, hoping at last to be introduced.

"I mean," she said, laying an exquisitely manicured finger on my forearm, "*you*. I saw Opener of the Way, you see. It's a stirring film, Conway. I thought–"

"It bore no relation to what happened," I interrupted. "It was sensationalised–"

"But surely, Conway, it was sensationalised in order to attain a greater metaphorical truth?"

I snorted at this. "It was sensationalised to get a greater share of the box-office takings," I said. "It misrepresented the characters and motives of my friends, and trivialised their past traumas. As for how I was portrayed..."

She laid a hand on my arm, her touch electrifying, leaned close and whispered, "Well, perhaps during my stay here I will get to know the real David Conway, yes?"

I smiled, and mumbled something.

"Anyway, what do you do with yourself these days, Conway?"

"Ah..." I opened my mouth, shrugged, and smiled stupidly. How I hated questions like these. In the months following the opening of the way, five years ago, reporters from across the Expansion had hot-footed it to Chalcedony to ask me similarly inane questions, expecting me to have made fabulous wealth, and be living in some palatial beachfront mansion. I think they were disappointed with what they found; a reticent, middle-aged beach-bum who liked nothing more than reading books and relaxing in the company of a select group of friends.

I decided to be honest. "I do nothing, other than read, and walk, and enjoy drinking with friends."

Her reaction surprised me. I had expected her to be disappointed. "Do you know something, Conway? That sounds like the perfect sort of life, to me."

I nodded. "I'm happy."

"Happiness..." she said, and a faraway look came into her eyes.

I glanced towards the far end of the room. "Ah... who are the other guests?" I asked.

Luna returned to the present with a grim smile. "The three upright and handsome gentlemen are all my ex-husbands, Conway."

I opened my mouth, tried to think of a suitable response, and failed.

"The blonde Nordic type is Bjorn Hansen, the explorer. I married him when I was far too young, just eighteen, and lived to regret the fool I was. To his right, the balding black man is Rudolph Carter, the banker." She leaned close to me again. "I was twenty when I made *that* mistake. He was a sadist, and one of the finest. Physical and psychological – an expert. Needless to say, it didn't last long."

I stared at the group, aware that there was something strange about them, which I couldn't quite put my finger on. "And the last one?"

"The tall, dark Latino is Edward Rodriguez, the actor. Another catastrophe. How was I to know he preferred boys, and only wanted me as a trophy?"

The odd thing, I thought, was that while we'd be talking about them, only the length of the room away, not once had they glanced in our direction. Seconds later I realised another odd thing: they all appeared to be roughly the same age, in their thirties – and yet if Luna had married Hansen when she was only eighteen...

Luna trilled a laugh. "I can see that you're confused, Conway! Come on, I'll introduce you." She knocked back her drink and moved, unsteadily, towards the trio of failed husbands. I took her elbow, lest she trip on the plush carpet, and steered her across the room.

She paused before the group. "Now, which one of you... you detestable bastards will admit–" she hiccuped "–that you're a bunch of self-centred, arrogant, talentless nothings?"

I looked away, knowing that I must have appeared the epitome of embarrassment.

I glanced at the girl, who stood a couple of metres away, demurely nursing a drink – but she failed to return my look. I wondered, briefly, who among the three men was her father: she appeared in her twenties, with raven hair and mocha skin: Rodriguez, then?

I glanced back at the group. Amazingly, not one of Luna's ex-husbands deigned to be baited.

Luna laughed again, crossed to a small, matte black console mounted on the wall, and touched a sensor panel.

Instantly, the three men winked out if existence.

The girl remained, turning and smiling at Luna.

"Holo-projections..." I said to both of them.

Luna waved, a little drunkenly, at where the trio had stood. "I like to keep them around, Conway, to remind me of my failures – to remind me to be more careful in future, to never act impulsively in matters of the heart, to be... to be wary. Oh, Christ, how I wish I'd had the ability to see into the future, Conway. Wouldn't that be a blessing?"

I said, uneasily, "I'm not sure. If one could see one's mistakes, and yet be unable to do anything about them..."

"But," she said, leaning close to me and almost toppling, "but that's just it, Conway. If you could see your mistakes before they happened, then you'd be able to stop yourself from making them, yes?"

I hesitated, not wanting to get into a debate about determinism with an unhappy and obviously distraught woman.

As if seeking refuge, I turned to the girl and said, "What do you think?"

The girl stared at me, through me.

Luna laughed again. "She doesn't think anything, Conway. She is stupid. You see, that's me when I was twenty-five. I'd just divorced Rodriguez and was at the height of my fame." She reached for the wall.

And the girl, like all the others, vanished at the touch of a switch.

Five

"And not long after that," I told my friends the following morning as we drove towards the central massifs, "she collapsed in a drunken heap and I made my escape."

"And she didn't explain herself, or apologise?" Maddie asked.

I laughed. "That's why she invited me over, isn't it? I'd completely forgotten about that. No, she didn't say a word about her behaviour on the beach the other morning."

"She sounds," Hawk said, from the passenger seat beside Matt, "a sad and tragic woman."

I nodded. "She's haunted by who she was, the mistakes she made."

"But what's she doing on Chalcedony?" Maddie asked.

"That I didn't get round to discussing."

Matt laughed. "You can ask her the next time she invites you round for a drink, David."

I returned his laugh with a hollow version of my own and concentrated on the passing scenery. What I'd neglected to tell my friends was that, immediately after she'd extinguished the ghosts of her past, she had taken my hand and dragged me towards a nearby sofa. There, she'd traced a long finger down my cheek and asked me if I realised what a handsome man I was. Fortunately, as she leaned towards me with predatory lips, she'd lost consciousness and collapsed back against the cushions, and *then* I had fled.

Now I recalled that Hawk had known one of her old lovers. I said, "Did you ever meet Carlotta when you knew... what was

31

his name, the pilot?"

"Grainger," Hawk said. "No – he talked about her plenty, but I never met the woman. I only knew Grainger briefly. We flew a couple of missions together." He lapsed into silence.

I watched the shola trees flicker past, thought about last night, and tried to work out my reluctance to get involved with Carlotta Chakravorti-Luna. There was no denying that she was beautiful, and famous, and no doubt rich – and many a man would have fallen at her feet, given the opportunity. But I think I saw her as an unwelcome interruption of a contented life; I was happy for the first time in years, and Luna, with her complicated past and twisted emotional freight, would have been an unnecessary burden.

Beside me, Maddie said, "A penny for them, David."

I decided to come clean. "Before I left last night, Luna made a pass at me – then collapsed. I was just wondering why I don't want anything to do with her."

Maddie regarded me, and with her usual perceptiveness said, "It's because you haven't had a relationship for over five years, David, and you're afraid she'd find you wanting."

I opened my mouth to protest, then shut it and smiled.

That morning, before setting off, Matt had rung around every car-hire franchise in MacIntyre, asking if they'd rented a vehicle at any time in the past five days to a single female Ashentay. He'd drawn a blank at a dozen places, and then struck lucky. A small firm on the edge of town had hired out an off-road bison to a native, two days ago. Which meant that Kee would have already reached the sacred site.

One hour later we turned off the highway and took a winding minor road through the rucked foothills. Ahead, the central massifs were scintillating facets of purple rock topped by snow, their lower slopes cloaked in jungle.

As we drove, I thought about Hawk and the alien girl. Many human relationships were hard to fathom, but trying to work out the mutual attraction between a fifty-five year-old space pilot and an alien almost half his age was impossible. It was easy to be glib about it and see what Hawk saw in Kee: she was, after all, young and pretty in a fey, elfish kind of way. As to what she saw in him... I'd once asked her about her relationship with Hawk (I was drunk at the time) and she'd merely smiled and said, "Hawk is a good man. In the words of my people, he and I are *k'oto*." And when I asked what that meant, in English, she had merely smiled again and shook her head gently. "There is no word in English, David."

But I saw how Hawk and Kee behaved together, and I could not doubt their love.

We climbed. The road became twistier, and the drop to our left took on a frightening aspect. I'd never been good with heights and I tried not to look. This far inland the vegetation was spectacular compared to the littoral flora of the bay. We passed great multi-coloured blooms that looked like fireworks made flesh, riotous fountains of sparkling leaf and bud. The open-top car was flooded with a heady, honeyed scent.

Maddie pointed far ahead, beyond the mountains. Through the mist, we could just make out the effulgence of the Yall's golden column, the alien construct which, until five years ago and our discovery, had remained one of the Expansion's greatest mysteries.

Maddie said, "It doesn't seem like five years, does it? Do you know something, I never thought we'd survive intact, as a group of friends, after all the media interest."

"What?" I looked at her. "Did you think we'd be lured by all the offers, the money? The fame?"

She smiled. "When Hawk decided to pilot a ship through the column to the stars... I thought that was the start of the break-up. And then the film offers came in."

"Which we all refused to have anything to do with," I pointed out.

33

"Yes, and how I loved you all for telling the money men to go stuff themselves!" Maddie said. "Little did we realise that the unauthorised film would be so terrible…"

Hawk turned in his seat. "But how do you think the experience *did* change us?"

"Well," I said, "we all learned something about ourselves, didn't we? We grew. I think we became stronger. Happier. I know I did."

Maddie reached forward and mussed Matt's hair. "And I found the man of my dreams, didn't I, deary?"

Matt just laughed.

"And I found I could pilot again," Hawk said. "Strange thing was, after a few trips out-there, that was enough. To know that I could do it. What mattered was what I had here on Chalcedony, my friends, and Kee."

At this he lapsed into silence again, and our thoughts returned to the alien girl.

An hour later Matt slowed to a stop and indicated the screen on the dashboard. "Dar is twenty kilometres south-west of here," he said. "There are no metalled roads indicated, and the track isn't shown on this." He shrugged. "Any idea where it might be, Hawk?"

"Let's drive a little further and keep a look out," Hawk suggested.

Matt started the engine and we drove south-west, keeping our eyes peeled for a break in the jungle to our right. Thirty minutes later Maddie called out, "There!"

A sandy track, little wider than the car itself, interrupted the wall of vegetation. "And look," she went on, pointing.

A series of saddled hills could be seen beyond the treetops, and kilometres away, nestling in a green clearing between two rearing peaks, stood a collection of huts. Smoke drifted vertically, undisturbed by wind. I made out the tiny stick-figures of alien natives.

"Dar," Hawk said.

Matt eased the car right, squeezing between the trees. Fronds whipped by, lashing at us. The jungle panoply closed in and the sunlight diminished. We bucked along the uneven track at walking pace.

Matt said, "When we reach the village – if we reach the village – we'll have to leave the car and continue on foot. How far did you say the sacred site was from Dar?" he asked Hawk.

"Roughly ten kilometres."

"Hell of a walk," I said.

The jungle opened out as we climbed, and the track widened. We no longer had to dodge the attention of lashing branches and fronds. Matt picked up speed. I gazed up at the tranquil view of the sequestered alien village and wondered how the locals might receive us – how indeed they might view our quest to retrieve the alien girl before she indulged in what the Ashentay saw as a valid cultural ritual?

I voiced my concern.

Hawk said, "We won't tell them we want to stop her. We'll just say we need to find her. The Ashentay aren't a curious people. They won't ask questions. It'll help that I can speak a little of their language. Thing is, we might be too late."

Maddie said, "Even if we are, Hawk, then look at it realistically – chances are that Kee will be okay."

"I know, statistically. But even so…"

I said, "But if we find her before she's taken part in the ritual, how will she react to us barging in and saying she shouldn't do it?"

Hawk grunted a laugh. "Kee's stubborn. But I'll tell her that what she's doing will hurt me, pain me, and that might make her think again."

"But," Matt pointed out, "she's obviously doing it for a reason. She's a sensitive person, Hawk; she'll have thought through the consequences."

Hawk nodded. "I know, I know. And that's what makes it all the more painful." He stopped there, then said, "I'd just like to know why she feels she has to go through with it, is all."

We had no answer to that, and we fell silent as the car rocked and careered along the pot-holed track.

Ten minutes later Matt slowed down and said, "Look."

"Jesus," Hawk said.

A hundred metres ahead, to our right, sunlight glinted off the roof of a bison. It had gone off the track, into the ditch, and fetched up against the thick bole of a palm. It all depended, I thought, on how fast the vehicle had been travelling when it impacted with the tree.

It occurred to me that if she had crashed the vehicle a couple of days ago, injured herself and was still in there... She was a slight creature, almost childlike. I felt my pulse increase as we approached.

Hawk was leaning forward, and I was glad I was unable to make out his expression.

Matt slowed and braked beside the canted bison.

Maddie said, "Are you sure it's Kee's?"

Hawk just pointed to the hire-car logo on the door of the vehicle.

We climbed out. The bison's fender was buckled, the windscreen shattered. There was no sign of Kee. Hawk yanked open the passenger door and climbed inside. I peered in after him.

He was staring at the blood on the dashboard; he gave a low groan. Maddie took his arm and helped him away from the cab; I climbed inside. Matt rounded the vehicle and approached it from the driver's side. He stared at me through the open door.

"It's my guess this makes it seem worse than it is," I said, loud enough so that Hawk could hear. "The driver's door is open. I reckon she climbed out."

I scrambled from the cab and joined Matt. He was staring at

the broken vegetation in the ditch beside the truck.

"She went this way," he said, indicating a patch of trampled grass. He moved away from the bison, along the ditch, then climbed out onto the track. I followed him.

He indicated the sandy surface of the road. I made out patches of what looked like scarlet sugar – Kee's spilled blood that had picked up grains of sand and dried in globules.

Matt called back to Hawk. "She survived the crash and walked away." He looked up and fitted his hand over his eyes, shielding the sunlight. "I think she made for the village."

Hawk joined us, Maddie by his side. We followed the sporadic trail of blood along the road until it petered out. Maddie said, "I don't think she was bleeding all that badly."

"Badly enough," Hawk said, "going by the mess in the cab."

"She'll be fine," I said. "It's not far to the village. Look at it this way, it might even have slowed her down. She might not have made the ritual yet."

Hawk nodded. "Let's get going."

We climbed back into Matt's car and set off again, driving slowly and from time to time coming almost to a stop in order to scan the ground and search the ditch.

I glanced at Maddie. She looked white. I wondered if we were putting an optimistic gloss on the evidence: there was always the chance that Kee had been badly injured in the accident and had wandered off into the jungle, but I kept my thoughts to myself.

The track climbed and wound around a hillside, and twenty minutes later we turned a bend and before us was Dar, a collection of perhaps fifty straw-hatted huts dotting the green incline.

Matt braked a hundred metres before the first hut and suggested we go the rest of the way on foot. We nodded agreement and climbed out. Hawk was expressionless, his stony features set.

Our arrival had been noted by a group of children playing on the perimeter of the village. They stopped and watched us, frozen into comical immobility, before running off twittering into the village. Seconds later the adults gathered, though these people seemed hardly taller than their children.

They were a humanoid race, almost identical to *Homo sapiens* to the point where they might have gone unnoticed in a crowd of humans. You might have wondered, though, at their slightness, their wide mouths, thin noses and large eyes; their faces bordered on the ugly, but in a few instances, as with Kee, possessed a strange and delicate beauty.

We advanced slowly and stopped perhaps ten metres from the gathered group. Hawk stepped forward, a hand raised in a gesture of greeting. He halted, cleared his throat, and spoke in their language. It seemed odd, a series of mellifluous, almost watery notes coming from the mouth of this rangy, piratical figure.

An old man pushed his way through the grouped aliens and stood staring at the ground, his head cocked in an attitude of polite attention.

When Hawk fell silent, there was a stirring among the Ashentay, and all eyes turned to the elder. He wore nothing but a loin-cloth and a necklace of beads; his face, despite the lines, suggested vitality.

Hawk turned to us and whispered, "I asked if they know of a fellow Ashentay called Kee, who had crashed a vehicle nearby and might have made her way to the village."

The old man spoke quickly, and I glanced at Hawk. He nodded, frowning as he attempted to decipher the elder's fluid tongue.

Hawk said to us, "He asked what business it is of ours."

He spoke to the elder again; I caught the word 'Kee' from time to time.

There was a stirring of interest among the group. Hawk said,

"I told them that Kee was a dear friend of ours, and that she came to the area intending to take part in the smoking of bones ritual, but that she had crashed her vehicle before arriving here. I said we're concerned for her safety."

The elder moved his hand in a quick, circular gesture and spoke.

He was still speaking when Hawk hung his head and said, under his breath, "Thank Christ..." He turned to us, relief flooding his face. "She's okay. She came to them two days ago. She had a badly cut forehead, and her arm was injured. But Jyrik – the elder – he said the village's doctor fixed her up and she left the village on foot today."

"Today?" Maddie said. "How early?"

Hawk spoke to the elder, then reported, "She set off at first light."

"And how far is it to the sacred site?" Maddie asked.

Hawk addressed the elder again.

The old man flung out a hand towards the mountains and uttered a flow of whispery words.

"A few hours," Hawk relayed, unable to keep the smile from his face.

Maddie said, "Then we might catch up with her before..."

"If we follow in the car," I said.

Hawk was shaking his head. "I asked him about the terrain. The car wouldn't stand a chance–"

"What about the bison?" Matt said. "I could go back and see what state it's in..."

Hawk spoke with the elder, then said, "It's worth a try. It's pretty steep terrain, but we could go as far as possible and travel the rest of the way on foot. The elder said he'd provide a guide."

"We'll go back to the bison," Matt said. "Try to get it started."

While Hawk continued his conversation with the elder, Matt, Maddie and I hurried back to the car. Matt jumped into the driver's seat and we sped back down the track. Ten minutes later we came to the bison.

Matt hoisted himself into the cab while I moved to the rear of the vehicle and inspected the ditch; it wasn't deep, and I suspected the bison's tracks would have no difficulty in reversing out.

I joined Matt and Maddie in the cab. Matt held up the ignition card, kissed it and said, "Now let's just hope the smash didn't do any irreparable damage."

He inserted the card and depressed the starter, and the engine roared to life. The bison bucked, and Matt yelled and hauled the gear-lever into reverse. With much revving and swearing, he eased the vehicle from the ditch and pointed it in the direction of the village.

We bucketed along, laughing like kids on a fairground ride.

By the time we reached the village, Hawk was unloading provisions from the car. We stowed them aboard the bison and climbed back into the cab. Hawk remained standing beside the vehicle, discussing – I presumed – the matter of directions with the elder. A minute later a young female Ashentay climbed warily into the passenger seat beside Hawk; her resemblance to Kai, to my untutored eye, was remarkable. She glanced unsurely at him, and then back at us, and reached out to touch the unfamiliar lines of the cab with timid wonder.

We left the village, crashing along a track through the enclosing jungle, and began to climb.

As Hawk wrestled with the steering wheel, almost manhandling the bison through the steep terrain, he spoke to the girl.

She replied with monosyllables at first, hardly glancing at him. Then, as he gained her trust, she smiled and chattered more easily.

Over his shoulder, Hawk reported, "Qah says that Kee went with a group of Ashentay, whose time it also was to smoke the bones. They were impressed that she'd come so far by herself, and they wanted to know more about her life with us humans. I don't think she told them she was living with me; some tribes might ask how that came about, and if they found out... well, they'd probably shun her."

The fact was that, ten years ago, Kee had been left in the jungle by her family as an offering to the Koah tree; she was the youngest girl from a litter of twenty children, and therefore expendable, and great credit would accrue to her tribe when her spirit was absorbed by the holy tree.

Then Hawk had happened along and rescued her, and the rest was history.

He said, "I asked her how many of her tribe had undergone the smoking ritual over the years. She said perhaps a hundred, with around thirty fatalities." He looked grim.

"Don't worry," Maddie said. "We'll get to her before it starts."

We held on as the bison rocked back and forth, riding the motion like sailors on a storm-tossed sea. The jungle swamped us, filtering the light to an aqueous gloom. I heard the eerie squeals of alien fauna and wondered if there were any predatory animals in the region.

Hawk answered my question. "We're safe. The hoffa live on the southern continent and never get this far north. There are some nasty insects, though, and snake analogues... I just hope it doesn't come to leaving the bison and walking."

He spoke to the Qah, who replied.

He called back to us, "I asked her how far away the sacred site is, in distance, not days spent walking. She said twelve toha, say about eight kay. We should make it in a few hours. Before sunset, at any rate."

The Fates must have been attending to his words. Two hours later the incline, already steep, reared to a forty-five degree slope and the bison growled, dug in, butted aside a few thickboled trees, and finally admitted defeat. Hawk tried again and again, backing up and charging at the obstruction, then attempting to go around it, but to no avail.

"I think this is as far as we go," he said. "The rest of the way is on foot."

Qah leapt nimbly from the cab, manifestly relieved to be back in an environment she understood. She ran ahead, making light work of the incline, stood on a toppled tree trunk and stared ahead.

She called something to Hawk, who translated. "She says it's not far from here. An hour or so. If we hurry, we'll make it by nightfall."

We hauled backpacks containing tents, water and food from the bison and followed our guide, Hawk first, Maddie and Matt coming after, and myself bringing up the rear. It was hot, the kind of sultry heat that has one drowning in sweat after about five seconds of exertion. I looked ahead, through the thick cover of foliage; the sun was making its slow descent towards the near, mountainous horizon.

The going, surprisingly, was not as difficult as I'd expected. We'd followed a narrow path in the bison, the vehicle widening it somewhat, and we continued on it now. The sandy trail climbed through the jungle, affording occasional glimpses through the canopy of the rearing peaks ahead.

The climb might have been easier than I'd feared, but I still found the going hard. Muscles which I'd forgotten I possessed began to protest, and my lungs felt as if they were being forced up through my gullet.

We'd been walking for an hour when Maddie looked over her shoulder and smiled. "You okay back there?"

I grinned heroically. "I'm still here, Maddie," I panted. "Surely there can't be much further to go?"

As if he'd heard me, Hawk called a halt. We gathered on a mossy rise and, after speaking with Qah, he pointed through a rent in the canopy ahead. "See that hill, projecting from the jungle? The waterfall to the right? That's where we're heading. Thirty minutes, no more."

"Hallelujah," I laughed. I broke out my water canister and took a long drink. The others did the same.

"The gym for you, my boy, when we get back," Maddie threatened.

We set off again, our lithe guide skipping ahead, making the incline seem like child's play.

The sun was slipping behind a jagged mountain peak when we crested a rise and saw, a few hundred metres ahead, a domed hill rising before us with a quicksilver waterfall cascading from the rocks to the right.

"This is it?" Matt asked. "The sacred site?"

I looked for signs of occupation, huts or temples or something, but the place seemed deserted.

Hawk said, "Behind the waterfall is the entrance to a system of caves. The rituals are performed in one of these caverns. Qah suggested that we spend the night by the waterfall; she said she'll enter the caves and look for Kee..." He shook his head. "I told her we need to find Kee sooner rather than later. We'll go into the caves and follow Qah to the sacred chamber."

"And she's okay with this?" Maddie asked.

Hawk nodded. "She seems to be. As far as I know there's no precedent ever been set of humans entering sacred territory, so..."

"Let's go," Matt said.

We crossed the clearing, and the humidity seemed to lift as we left the confines of the jungle; a flagging wind lapped across the hill, and as we approached the waterfall its spray drenched us in a cool, jewelled shower.

Qah led us around the sink formed by the waterfall, and along a ledge behind its sheer crystal sheet of water. The rock underfoot was treacherous, and Matt, Maddie and I gripped each other's hands as we inched along the ledge.

We came to a gaping rent in the rock and followed Qah within. Something glowed on the walls, mats and rafts of what looked like fungus, giving off a dull green luminescence.   We followed a natural corridor in the rock as it dropped rapidly. I made out carvings on the walls, stick Ashentay figures and animals, and wondered what xenologists back on Earth would make of this alien treasure.

Ten minutes later I saw light ahead, brighter than the verdant gloaming of the corridor. Seconds later we emerged into a vast cavern.

I thought, for a second, that we had emerged into the twilight, that we'd somehow penetrated through to a valley fissure deep within the mountain. Then my eyes adjusted and I made out the rocky bounds of the cavern – perhaps a kilometre distant – and the fires, bonfires no less, situated at intervals around the perimeter and providing a bright rouge glow. Only then did I make out the long-house, raised on stilts above the ground and entered by a timber ramp. Positioned in the centre of the pitched roof was an opening through which poured a thick pall of smoke. It rose and hung beneath the natural ceiling of the chamber like a threatening storm-cloud.

I inhaled and smelled the sweet, almost familiar scent of the bone smoke.

Six

We were standing on a slightly raised gallery, looking down. A dozen Ashentay stood at the foot of the ramp to the long-house, and though they were perhaps only fifty metres from us, so far we had not been seen.

Then we heard an inhuman squealing, and three Ashentay males struggled from a pen behind the long-house. They were wrestling with a black-pelted beast the size of a rhino though more resembling a terrestrial pig, but for its deadly array of horns and a spiked tail which whipped back and forth as the creature attempted to escape.

Its captors delivered the creature to their waiting fellows, and two women stepped forward with long knives and sliced into the beast's thick neck. Blood geysered and the animal's dying squeal turned to a guttering splutter as it lay twitching on the rock. Then the butchers set to work and seconds later the flesh had been flensed. Four Ashentay men stepped forward, intoned something above the jackstraw scatter of bones, then bundled them up, climbed the ramp to the long-house and passed inside.

Qah spoke in a hushed, reverent tone.

"The ritual of sacrifice," Hawk said. "The gheer donates its bones for the ritual of smoking."

Maddie said, "So it hasn't taken place yet?"

Hawk spoke to Qah. She replied, and he reported, "She doesn't know. She said she'll try to find out."

Qah called out and hurried down to the gathered Ashentay.

An old man, tall for an Ashentay, stepped from the long-house holding an intricately carved spear. On his head he wore a

45

long wooden mask, with wide staring eyes and a rictus grin; the headpiece was topped with an array of gheer horns.

He paused in the entrance at the top of the ramp, then moved to one side and dropped his spear with a great thump on the timber floor.

As if at this signal, six Ashentay males emerged from the long-house. They walked carefully down the ramp in pairs, bearing laden stretchers.

"Christ…" Hawk turned to us. "They're bringing out the dead…"

I stared at the figure on the first stretcher; it appeared female, but as one Ashentay looked very much like any other I was unable to say whether or not she might have been Kee.

Hawk staggered forward, and we followed. We slowed our approach, something like respect, or a desire to be seen not to be intruding, curbing our haste. We paused before the long-house and the stretcher-bearers passed us without any suggestion that they might have been disconcerted by our presence. I stared at the body on the first stretcher and saw that it was not Kee.

On the second stretcher was the body of a male Ashentay, and on the third…

I took a step forward, peering intently. It was a woman, but not Kee.

I heard Hawk choke back a relieved sob, and Maddie and Matt moved to his side.

I peered into the shadows of the building, and made out several shadowy figures. Seconds later, the survivors of the smoking ritual emerged one by one.

They ducked from the long-house and straightened, blinking in the half-light after the darkness. They wore the rapt expressions of religious devotees who had been granted glimpses of their destinies.

I scanned the aliens as they stepped down the ramp. I thought I saw Kee – a slight, fine-boned young girl… Hawk took a step forward and reached out, his expression of nascent hope collapsing as the girl approached and passed him by.

By my count twelve aliens – including the dead trio – had emerged from the long-house.

Maddie murmured, "But where is Kee?"

Qah moved to Hawk's side and indicated a dozen seated cross-legged between the distant bonfires. They stood as one and crossed the cavern to the long-house. In the doorway, the priest thumped his spear on the timber threshold and called out.

Hawk said, "Kee..." and only then did I make out her slight figure, third in line, and I understood.

"Christ..." Hawk said. "It's time for the next intake. I've got to go through all that again!"

The dozen Ashentay approached the long-house. Kee paused, then deviated from her route and came to Hawk. She laid a tiny hand on his tanned forearm and whispered in English, "This I must do, Hawk."

He shook his head. "I don't understand. Aren't you happy with what we've got?"

She gave a sad smile, perhaps at his incomprehension. "Of course I am happy; I have never been happier. But there comes a time when we must look ahead, and give thanks to our creator that we have the opportunity to perceive what the future holds."

"But I don't see why, what benefit..." Hawk began. "And the danger. Kee, I don't want to lose you!"

She reached up and touched his cheek, having to stand on tip-toe to do so. "We must accept, Hawk. Isn't that what life is about, after all? An acceptance, an accommodation with one's fate?"

"No!" Hawk began.

The old man barked a peremptory command.

Kee smiled at Hawk once more and made to move.

Hawk took her by the shoulders, pulled her to him and held her. The disparity between her elfin slimness and his ursine solidity would have been comical, were it not so tragic. He was weeping, and she closed her eyes and accepted his embrace with an expression of infinite calm.

He let her go, reluctantly, and she turned and followed her fellows up the ramp, and disappeared into the shadows of the long-house.

Qah approached Hawk and spoke to him. He nodded and replied.

"What?" Maddie asked.

"The ritual could take as long as ten, twelve hours," he said. "I'm staying here–"

Matt said, "Hawk, there's nothing you can do. You'd be torturing yourself. Look, let's go back to the clearing, set up camp. I have some imported whiskey. We could eat, have a drink..."

"Matt's right," Maddie said. "There's absolutely nothing we can do here. Let's get something to eat, and we'll get back here well before the ritual's ended."

Hawk looked at the long-house, his expression stricken. I took his shoulder and shook him. "C'mon, Hawk. I've never known you turn down a meal."

Hawk nodded, then spoke to Qah. She replied, and he translated, "She said she'll come and find us when the ritual's nearly finished."

We made our way from the chamber and back up the narrow tunnel to the waterfall. The sun had set and the Ring of Tharssos was illuminating the sheer fall of water so that it looked, as we emerged, like some expensive lighting effect. Carefully we moved along the ledge and out onto the clearing. The Ring was a vivid slash of silver arcing across the heavens, and beyond it I made out the bright scatter of stars.

Matt fetched our backpacks from where we'd dumped them and we set up camp.

It was a warm night, so we elected not to erect the domes

but to sleep out in the open. Matt fixed a meal and broke out the promised whiskey, and we sat around in a circle and ate and drank.

Matt chatted about the project he was working on now, the emotion spheres, and how he hoped they would eventually go on tour around the Expansion. I always enjoyed listening to Matt talk shop. I glanced at Hawk; he was watching Matt but his expression was distant as he gripped his glass, taking measured sips from time to time.

After the meal, and after we'd worked our way halfway down the bottle, Matt rolled out the inflatable sleeping bags and we turned in. Matt and Maddie lay together, Hawk beside them and myself at the end. I lay and stared at the scintillating stars.

Hawk said, as if to himself, "It's all so bloody primitive! Why put yourself at such stupid risk? Who the hell wants to know what the future has in store, anyway?"

Maddie said, "They are different, Hawk. You know that. You must respect their ways."

Hawk said, "I know, Maddie. I know that. But even so… Christ, if I lost her, I honestly don't know what I'd do."

Matt said, "She'll be fine, Hawk. I know it."

Hawk fell silent, and I slipped into sleep.

I was awoken twice, once by Hawk muttering in his sleep, and much later by a noise to our left. I rolled over and stared across the clearing. The light of the Ring was sufficient to illuminate a procession of tiny, fine-boned aliens – their chatter like the babble of running water – as they made their way towards the sacred caverns. The next dozen participants in the smoking ritual, I thought, before drifting off again.

* * *

I awoke shortly before dawn to find Maddie pushing at my shoulder. "David, get up. It's time."

49

I groaned and rolled over. Qah stood beside Hawk, who was struggling into his jacket. "She says the ritual's almost over. We'd better get going."

I washed the sleep from my eyes with a canister of water, and Maddie handed out bottles of juice. We drank as we hurried through the warm dawn, the sun rising bloody at our backs and sending our elongated shadows stretching ahead.

Qah led the way along the ledge behind the waterfall, Hawk close on her heels. I followed Matt and Maddie, dread lodged in my heart. What if Kee had succumbed to the smoke? I contemplated the prospect, and I wondered if some compensatory fate was about to strike, equalising the balance: we'd had a fine few years together as a group of friends, victim of neither tragedy nor hardship. Perhaps this was when the good times came to a terrible end.

I tried to banish the treacherous thought as we dropped through the tunnel. Hawk hurried towards the arched entrance and the sacred chamber, no longer needing Qah to lead the way. We almost ran to catch up.

Nothing had changed in the cavern. Night or day had no effect here. The bonfires maintained a constant, ruddy light. Beside the long-house, the stretcher-bearers waited passively. We might have gone back in time to when we had first entered the sacred site, but for the collective fear and apprehension that gripped us as we approached the foot of the ramp.

We had an agonising fifteen minutes to wait before there was movement from within the long-house. Hawk was all for striding up the ramp and ending the agony, but something Qah said, a quick fluting command, stopped him. Maddie took his hand and Matt murmured a few consolatory words.

The tall priest emerged at the top of the ramp, stood to one side like a carved statue, and thumped his spear.

The sense of apprehension was almost tangible.

Seconds later the stretcher-bearers hurried up the ramp and

ducked through the entrance. Half a minute later the first pair emerged, walking with dignity and care as they negotiated the opening with the laden stretcher. Hawk gave a moan as they moved down the ramp. I was beside him as the bearers passed us by, and we stared at the figure of the dead alien.

It was a young male, and I felt a sudden surge of relief, followed by a quick sense of guilt.

Beside Hawk, Matt squeezed his hand.

The stretcher-bearers unloaded their burden, laying the body reverently on a stone slab beside the long-house.

Hawk turned to Qah and spoke quickly. She replied, but could not bring herself to meet his eyes.

"Jesus," Hawk said, turning to us as if in appeal. "There's another three dead in there!"

Maddie said, "Can't you ask her if she knows whether...?"

Hawk shook his head. "I asked. She says she isn't allowed to enquire."

I knew, then, with an odd, cold certainty, that Kee would be among the dead, and I thought ahead to how we might be able to help Hawk through his time of grief. Hard upon that thought came the recollection of my own loss, six years ago, and a selfish part of me did not want to be reminded of that all over again.

There was movement in the shadows of the entrance. The next stretcher-bearers emerged. This time, I saw, the dead alien was that of a young female. I shut my eyes, feeling tears start, hot and raw.

I heard the sound of feet on the giving timbers of the ramp, and could not keep my eyes closed. I stared into the fair, beautiful features of the girl, serene in death, as she was carried past.

It was not Kee. Beside me, Hawk was weeping with a mixture, I guessed, of relief and terrible apprehension.

I wondered if fate was being cruel to him, prolonging his torment until the time the stretcher-bearers brought out the body of his beloved. Matt and Maddie were beside Hawk. I joined them, not wanting to be alone in any of this, and took Hawk's shoulder.

Movement in the long-house's entrance. The bearers stepped from the shadows. I felt the beat of my heart, thudding against my ribs. I heard Matt muttering something beside me, maybe a prayer. We stepped forward as one as the bearers came down the ramp.

The body was male, and I closed my eyes and squeezed Hawk's shoulder.

One more to go...

This is it, I thought. This is the terrible moment when everything is changed for ever.

My grip on Hawk became tighter. Matt and Maddie held him. We would be with Hawk when he beheld the fate of Kee, and we would help him through the dark days ahead.

He let out a pained breath as the stretcher-bearers came into sight at the top of the ramp. They negotiated the ramp, slowly. I stared at the slight figure they carried. It was female, and golden, and beautiful, and it came to me what a farce this was, this slaughter of innocents all in the name of some inane alien religion.

And beside me Hawk gave a sob and collapsed again Matt, and I stared into the serene features of the girl as she was carried past us.

It was not Kee.

* * *

Minutes later the survivors appeared. Kee was the third person down the ramp. She and Hawk came together into each other's arms with a sudden rush, as if magnetised. They held on to each other, rocking back and forth, for a long time.

I glanced across at Matt and Maddie, who were crying unashamedly, and I realised that I too was weeping with relief.

Kee disengaged and came first to Maddie and embraced her quickly, and then to Matt. She hurried over to me and smiled, and I thought I saw something in her eyes, a desire to say something, perhaps explain herself. She gave me a swift hug and returned to Hawk, who back-handed tears from his cheeks and said, "Okay, let's get the hell out of here."

He paused then and looked back at the long-house, at the tall figure of the Ashentay priest, who appeared to be staring down at us. I thought, for a second, that Hawk intended to approach the priest, or at least say something to him, but if so the moment passed and he turned and joined us.

We left the sacred cavern and climbed the tunnel to the surface of the planet. Sunlight dazzled us as we emerged behind the curtain of the waterfall and crossed to our encampment. We stowed our belongings, shouldered our packs, and began the long walk through the jungle to where we had left the bison.

Qah led the way, followed by Hawk and Kee who walked hand in hand through the undergrowth.

We reached the bison towards midday, and Matt volunteered to drive. He turned the bison from the felled trunks and manoeuvred it in the direction of the alien village. We set off, the vehicle rocking.

After a period of silence, Hawk said, "You don't know what torture you put me through, girl."

It was a few seconds before Kee replied. "It had to be done. It was ritual, the way my people do things. If we do not have ritual, then what do we have?"

We did not respond; it was one of those impossible, alien statements to which there are no correct answers.

Hawk asked, "But was it worth it? I mean, was it worth the risk to your life?"

Again Kee was contemplative, before saying, "Risk? What is risk? I knew what I was doing. If I died, then that would have been my destiny. It would have been a fact that had to be accepted, the way of things." I had heard her say this before, and thought it almost Buddhistic. *The way of things...*

"And did you see the future?" Hawk asked at last. I felt that he was straining to keep the sarcasm from his voice.

"I beheld many images," Kee replied quietly.

"But specifically?" Hawk asked, obviously frustrated.

"Specifically?" she returned.

"I mean, did you see... me and you, how things might go between us?"

She inclined her head. "Me and you. Yes. I saw the future, me and you." She paused, then went on, in a whisper, "We were together until the very end."

I looked at Hawk; he had his mouth open to ask the obvious question, but decided otherwise. Perhaps now, in company, was not the right time.

We came to the Ashentay village, and here Hawk and Kee elected to return together in the bison, while Maddie, Matt and I drove back in Matt's ground-effect vehicle.

"Well," Maddie said as we were under way, "I suppose you'd call that a happy ending."

"Christ, but I thought she was dead," I said.

"Me too," Matt agreed. "God knows how Hawk would have coped."

I thought about the ritual. "I wonder what it must be like, to be granted visions of supposed future happenings? I mean, what must reality be like for a people who believe this?"

Matt said, "They're alien, David. We'll probably have no idea how they perceive reality."

Maddie said, "How do our fellow human's perceive reality, Matt? That's a hard enough question to answer, without trying to fathom the psychology of aliens."

We arrived in Magenta Bay towards late afternoon and parked before the Jackeral to say our goodbyes: Hawk and Kee were heading off down the coast.

As we were about to go our separate ways, Kee left Hawk's side and embraced first Matt, then Maddie, and then me. She raised herself on her toes and, hugging me, whispered in my ear, "David, I must see you. I must tell you something, okay? I will be in touch."

She withdrew, and the look in her eyes counselled me to remain silent. I merely smiled like an idiot and watched them drive off.

I said goodbye to Matt and Maddie and made my way home, lost in thought.

Seven

The following evening I met Matt and Maddie in the Jackeral.

It was late; we'd finished our meals and were enjoying a drink on the verandah. Hawk, not surprisingly, had called Maddie and explained that he wouldn't be joining us tonight: he was spending the evening with Kee, who was exhausted after the ritual.

"You're pensive, David."

"I was thinking, Maddie – what it must be like to live with someone who's glimpsed the future."

Maddie pursed her lips. "Well, I wouldn't say Kee so much glimpsed the future, as... What did she say? That she's seen images of the future. I don't know, but perhaps those images are like the ones in a dream: elusive, fragmentary. Hard to make much sense of."

Matt pushed a hand through his greying curls and smiled. "Perhaps, like dreams, they need interpreting."

"I just hope that it doesn't come between Hawk and Kee," I said. "You know Hawk, Mr Practical. There are no shades of grey with our space pilot."

Maddie said, "They've been through worse than this and they're still together. They'll be fine."

We watched Delta Pavonis lower itself into the sea; the fiery globe was so vast and molten that I expected to hear the sizzle as it touched the horizon. I was forever reminded, at sunset on Chalcedony, of that passage in Wells where the Time Traveller visits the far future and beholds the bloated sun straddling the horizon.

57

I suggested another drink, but Matt and Maddie made their excuses and departed. I watched them step down from the verandah and walk hand in hand through sands as red as cayenne pepper, and around the bay towards Matt's place.

I thought of Hawk and Kee, cosy down in the junkyard, and I suppose a maudlin introspection came over me, a reflective mood taking in the past and my failed marriage, and the fact that I was alone now. At least, I am stating this with the benefit of hindsight: perhaps I overstate my self-pity in order to excuse – or explain – what happened later that evening.

I regarded my glass, which was almost empty. Being someone who finds it hard not to indulge, I have always considered an almost empty glass to be a wonderful thing, with its promise of more to come. It was only my third beer that evening, so I made my way to the bar and ordered a fourth.

I returned to the verandah; I would watch the sun ease itself into the sea, and as its apex vanished then I would meander home. I judged that event to be at least another beer away.

"You look, Conway, both drunk and miserable."

Surprised, I looked up. Carlotta Chakravorti-Luna was peering down at me from the advantage of her considerable height.

I hoisted my glass. "Only my second," I lied. "And I'm far from miserable. In fact I've never been happier."

"Would you mind terribly if I joined you?"

I indicated a chair beside mine, and Luna not so much sat down but allowed the seat to receive her – to appropriate another image from Wells. She held a long glass containing something virulently crimson, took a tiny sip and placed it on the table before us.

I was glad to see that she was more modestly attired tonight. She was wearing a black sleeveless dress, cut short, with a neckline that stopped just this side of decency.

"I saw you by yourself on the verandah, and thought I'd

better come over and apologise."

I smiled, wondering which of our two meetings her apology might cover.

"I was a little drunk," she went on, "and I was going through a blue period – hence the holo of the bastard quartet. I sometimes get like that, when I wonder about the past, wonder how I ended up like this..."

"Like this?"

She considered me, her generous lips twisted into a rosebud moue. "How I ended up, at my age, living alone on some backwater colony world twenty light years from Earth."

"There are worse places," I began.

"Oh, God, Conway, of course there are. But I was being metaphorical."

I found it hard to think metaphorically after four pints of strong beer, but I nodded anyway.

"Metaphorical." I repeated. "You're unhappy?"

She tipped her glass, and the scarlet poison slipped down her long, graceful neck. "Of course I'm bloody unhappy, Conway. But then I always have been unhappy. Isn't unhappiness the default state of being human?"

I considered saying something along the lines of it all depended on one's perspective, but realised that that would have sounded sanctimonious.

"Anyway, are you going to buy me another drink?"

I looked at her, and realised for the first time that evening how incredibly beautiful she was. "It will be my pleasure," I said, inclining my head like a bar-room gallant. "But what is it?"

"Something called a Magenta Special. Vodka and that strange fruit that grows around here."

I finished my drink and navigated my way to the bar, aware of the stares from a few of the locals.

When I returned, Luna was gazing out at the disappearing sun, her expression wistful. She nodded and took her drink without meeting my eyes.

"So... what brought you to Magenta?" I asked.

She turned her head and stared at me. "Do you really want to know, Conway, or are you merely being polite?"

"No, I'm intrigued. I mean, I presume you could have had your pick of exotic locations around the Expansion."

She shook her head. "I wanted somewhere quiet, beautiful, away from the rat-race."

"More or less why I came here," I said.

"That was after the death of your daughter, right? Or did the film misrepresent that, too?"

"No, it got that bit right. I wanted a fresh start. To think," I said, shaking my head, "that if I'd picked somewhere else..." I often frightened myself with the thought that my life could have been very different, were it not for my decision to come to Chalcedony.

"Then humanity would still be telemassing at great expense around the universe," Luna finished for me – except that that wasn't quite how I would have completed the sentence.

"Actually," I said, "to be honest I wasn't thinking about the golden column. I mean, it's great that we can now travel wherever at a fraction of the expense..." And the discovery had brought back the wonderful starships of my youth. "But I was thinking more about the fact that what happened five years ago helped me get over losing my daughter, and I also met a few great people."

"Loss," she said, with a kind of drunken, dreamy, reflective air. "We try to get over it in our own very different ways..."

I thought of the holo-projections of her ex-husbands, and the young girl she had been, and it came to me that she was not making a very good job of overcoming her particular loss.

Uncannily, she regarded me and said, "And if you think I'm referring to my bastard husbands, you're dead wrong, Conway."

I riposted with, "I was thinking of the holo of your younger self," and immediately regretted it.

Anger flared in her vast brown eyes. "She represents everything I was, Conway, and everything I lost."

I waved my glass. "For godsake, Carlotta. Have you looked in a mirror lately? You're probably the most beautiful women on the planet, for chrissake."

She sniffed. "Thank you for that, Conway. But beauty is only skin deep, to employ a cliché. Beauty, to someone who has lived with it all their life, doesn't matter as much as you might think."

I blinked. "Then the loss you were referring to...?"

She sighed. "Conway, for twenty years I was the highest paid holo star on Earth. I starred in some of the finest productions ever made. I loved acting; God, you can't imagine how much I *loved* to act." She fell silent.

"And?"

"And then it stopped."

"The parts stopped coming?"

She regarded me as if I were an insect. "Where have you been for fifteen years, Conway?"

"I lived a quiet life in British Columbia," I began in my defence.

"The industry collapsed," she went on. "No one wanted to make holo-movies any more, when for a fraction of the cost a small team could use the images of real life people and make, construct, holo-movies on computers."

"Ah," I said, comprehension dawning; I've never been the fastest.

"I did a bit of acting here and there, a little stage work. But never enough. I sold my image, just to keep my persona out there – in the vain hope that holo-movies would make a comeback and I'd still be bankable." She shook her head. "I've seen some of the computer-generated films 'starring' Carlotta Chakravorti-Luna, and they're appalling. They have no heart, no emotion, no humanity... They're dead, and that's because they don't use human beings any more. They're *dead*. And for a long time I thought I was dead, too."

It was a bravura cameo, and I felt like applauding. I even thought I detected the shimmer of a tear in the corner of those amazing eyes.

She sniffed, and sipped her drink, and then smiled at me in a strangely confiding way which said *don't-mind-my-histrionics* without quite saying so.

"And while I'm being so honest, Conway, shall I tell you the real reason I came to Chalcedony?"

I blinked. "The real reason?"

"The *real* reason," she repeated.

"I'd be... honoured," I said, and meant it.

She looked around, as if suddenly realising where she was and not liking the venue.

"But not here, okay? How about we go back to my place, hm?"

I looked at her, and something within my gut flipped like a landed fish.

"Yes... yes, that'd be great."

We finished our drinks, slipped from the verandah, and walked along the beach. She was more inebriated than I'd assumed, and I gripped her arm to assist her through the dunes that fronted her place. By the time we climbed the steps my arm was around her waist and she was leaning against me, her perfume filling my head.

The glass door slid open at her approach; low lighting came on and music began to play. I was glad to see, as we entered the low lounge, that we would not be joined by the holographic ghosts tonight.

Though in that I might have been mistaken; as she fixed me a beer and herself a gin sling, she asked, "Have you ever seen a holo-movie called Starship Fall, Conway?"

I shook my head. "I don't think I have."

She swayed over to the wall console, handing me the beer *en passant*, and touched a dial. "We needn't watch it, as such. It really is trite and sentimental, but it will help to explain something."

I nodded, at a loss to comprehend this latest twist.

At the back of the lounge, evidently the area set apart for the projection of films, a small starship travelled slowly through the void of space. I recognised it from my childhood forays to Vancouver spaceport: a Class II Stryker exploration vessel.

Luna curled herself into a sofa and patted the cushion beside her. "Sit down, Conway, and I'll tell you all about it."

I obeyed, and she leaned against me, folding her legs beneath her bottom and sipping her gin. I was pleasantly drunk, and I recall feeling none of the trepidation of two nights ago. Luna was a beautiful woman, and I'd been alone for five years, and that was all that seemed to matter.

She said, "Just after my third marriage ended in disaster, Conway, I met a dashing man called Ed Grainger. He was a starship pilot. He'd worked for the Greatorex Line piloting exploration vessels, years before we met. And then along came Telemass and he was out of a job. When I met him he was making the most of the situation; he'd earned enough over the years to buy his own small ship..." She pointed with her glass, sloshing gin, towards the screen: the Class II Stryker was now orbiting an unidentified planet. "He ran a small exploration business, reconnoitring the out of the way planets the Telemass organisation were too busy to bother about. There wasn't much work around, but it satisfied a craving."

I nodded and watched the film. The ship swooped low over the alien world, roaring silently across miles and miles of empty grassland.

"I met him around the time my own career in holo-movies was crashing down around me. I think we felt a mutual empathy, though of course he could still practice his trade... I was reduced to appearing in third-rate plays in bug-fuck nowhere, Idaho."

She sipped her drink and looked suddenly bitter.

I suppressed a belch and said, "What happened?"

"What happened?" Her eyes became distant. "We fell in love. I was ecstatically happy for a year. I thought I'd found it at last, the real thing, a man I could love and who genuinely loved me."

I winced, waiting for the punchline, the betrayal, the acrimony...

"But Ed…" She fell silent, lips pursed and held off-centre as she considered something long gone.

"Luna," I said, "if you don't want to tell me, that's fine."

She looked at me and smiled. "No, I want to tell you. That's why I dragged you here, Conway. So I could spill the beans." She stopped and laughed suddenly at her use of the odd phrase.

"But Ed…?" I prompted.

"He'd kept something from me. I mean, everything was great. We shared everything. We had so much in common, could talk for days on end, and the sex was spectacular… But then Ed would go into these… these fugue states, not so much depression as... as periods of intense introspection, when he'd shut himself away for a day or so and wouldn't talk to anyone, not even me."

I nodded, wondering where all this was leading.

"What was his problem?"

She looked at me steadily. "He was taking a drug, and had been for years."

I nodded again, feeling like a psychiatrist.

"The thing was, it wasn't a physically debilitating drug. He was fit and healthy... but it did things to his mind, altered his moods."

"What was it?"

She smiled wistfully. "Ed called it Cassandra."

"It didn't have a common name?"

"No. You see, Ed was the only human being taking the stuff."

I pulled a face. "Then how on Earth did he come across it?"

"He was exploring a planet for the Greatorex Line when he discovered a race of aliens. He stayed with them over a year, and in that time he came to know the aliens and participated in their rites. There was one certain drug they used, and it intrigued him. He asked if he might try it, and he did... and, well, he never stopped. He made sure he had a stock of the stuff when he left the planet, and periodically over the next ten years he used it... resulting in these periods of bleak introspection."

She stopped there and stared at the image playing out across the room; the starship spiralled down, coming to land with a quick curtsy of its ramrod stanchions in a green mountain meadow.

Much delayed, it came to me. I said, "And the planet was Chalcedony, right? And the drug..."

I stopped there. Cassandra...?

Had Ed Grainger participated in the Ashentay bone-smoking ceremony?

I said, "He smoked the bones, right? He saw... or he thought he saw... the future?"

Luna said nothing, but indicated the image with her glass.

I watched, as the aliens appeared around the ship, small, humanoid, blonde people. The Ashentay – or the director's idea of them.

"Ed told me all about it after we'd been together for about three months. I like to think it was because we shared everything, had no secrets. But I think the truth was that he'd sold the rights of his story to a production company in order to subsidise his explorations, and they were going to make a movie of his time on Chalcedony... and then everyone would know."

"I'm sorry," I said. "Is that why you two split–?"

"Of course not, Conway. I was in love, besotted. I could live with his taking the drug, his evasions. It was a relief at last when I found out the reason for his fugues." She paused, then smiled at me, pain in her eyes. "It was when his supply of the drug was

65

running out that the trouble started. He needed more of it to attain the same effect, and it had certain psychotic-inducing side-effects."

I said, "But... when the Ashentay take the drug, they claim they can see into the future...?"

Luna nodded, and a strand of jet hair fell across her face. She eased it away with the back of her hand, the gesture beautiful, and suddenly I wanted to reach out and take her in my arms. I felt her pain, her sadness... Was it arrogant of me to think that I might in some way be able to help her?

"That's right, Conway. They do, and do you know something, they're right. Ed saw into the future – oh, it wasn't as if everything was crystal clear and obvious. He had to..." She struggled to find the right word.

I thought of what Matt had said earlier, and supplied it, "Interpret?"

"Yes, he had to interpret the visions he was granted. You see, he was a deeply spiritual man, Conway. Not the all-action hero of common myth. He craved the ultimate religious experience."

I frowned. "But this drug, if he was granted visions of the future... then what he'd see was one reality – how the future would be, unalterable." I shook my head, my thoughts slowed by the alcohol. "I don't understand how anyone could live with *knowing* the course of future events."

Luna reached out, laid two long fingers on my forearm and said, "Ah, but Ed had a theory, Conway. He thought that the drug offered visions of not one set, determined future, but a range of *possible* futures – and, armed with the knowledge of these possible futures, he could steer a course towards those he saw as desirable, beneficial. He explained it all to me in terms of quantum physics, of a multitude of possibilities..."

I considered what I had witnessed in the sacred cavern. "But the danger... If Ed was taking this stuff over a period of years, then he was lucky it didn't kill him."

She nodded. "Ed was careful, David. He took small doses."

I said, "And when the drug finally ran out?"

Tears, huge silver tears like globules of mercury, slid from her eyes and rolled over her high cheek bones. It could have been another performance, but something told me the emotion was genuine.

"Then Ed returned to Chalcedony. He came back for more of the blessed drug. I begged him not to go, to seek help, try to kick the habit. But by this time he was well and truly hooked on the idea of engineering his destiny. He couldn't give it up, and the only answer was to return to Ashentay. Despite the danger."

I said, "The danger that the drug would kill him?"

"Thanks to one of these visions of the future, he knew there was a possibility he'd never come back from Chalcedony."

"He told you this?"

She smiled with bitterness. "Of course not."

"Then how...?" I began.

She drew a long sigh. "When the drug was running out, and Ed first suggested returning to Chalcedony... of course I wanted to know what was happening, what would happen. I wanted to know that we had a future together."

Things fell into place. "You took the drug?"

She hesitated, then nodded. "Just a couple of times. And I saw... I saw a future in which I would be without Ed, a terrible period of loneliness. I took it again, considering what Ed had told me about the futures it showed being only *possible* futures... but again I saw myself alone. That's when I begged Ed not to go. He ignored me, as I knew he would..."

The silence stretched. I wanted to know what happened, of course, but I was sober enough to know the question would be crass.

At last Luna said, "Ed set off for Chalcedony, and never came back." She nodded towards the screen. "That's what the movie is about, Ed's first time on Chalcedony, and his fateful return."

I said, after an interval, "And that's why you're here, Carlotta, to attempt to find out what happened to him?"

"I believe his ship is out there somewhere, in the central massifs. I think he crashed, so close to his goal. I want nothing more than to find the ship, say goodbye to Ed – to bring an closure to that part of my life." She looked at me. "Does that sound foolish, Conway?"

I smiled. "No," I said. "No, it sounds eminently sensible to me."

Then I reached out and took her face in my hand, stroking her cheek with my thumb. She leaned into my hand, smiling.

"Will you tell me something, Carlotta?"

She nodded, silently.

I recalled the scent of her the other morning, and then the reek of the bone smoke in the Ashentay's sacred site... and I said, "Are you still smoking the drug?"

She smiled, and shook her head, the movement restricted by my hand. "No, Conway. That time way back was more than enough."

I smiled. Call me a fool, but I believed her.

Then she said, in almost a whisper. "Conway, let's go to bed, okay?"

It had been a long five years, and a big part of me was like a fearful, first-time schoolboy all over again, but Carlotta was a beautiful woman, and I felt I'd come to know her in the short time we'd been together. And I trusted her.

She slipped from her dress, and I fumbled with her underwear while she removed my clothes. Then we stood, naked, and she took me in her hand, and I almost passed out with the sudden, exquisite thrill of her touch.

Eight

We saw each other, day and night, for the next few days. I showed Carlotta around Magenta, then drove her into the mountains to experience the rockpools which were continually filled by the crystal clear waterfalls that tipped from level to level. We swam in the cool water of the pools and made love as the sun set, before picnicking naked then driving back to the Bay and drinking in the Jackeral until the early hours.

I was deliriously happy, like some love-smitten teenager. Carlotta told me about her childhood, the supposedly privileged upbringing of a pampered child, which in reality was a soulless time of being looked after by hired nannies while her mother and father jetted around the world making their famous movies. She recounted her days as a holo-movie star, the paradox of believing in her art and yet despising most of the people in the industry.

In turn, I told Carlotta about my childhood in Vancouver, my obsession with space and the starships that crossed the void.

Those few days were a happy period, and the intimacy, the trust of another human being, made me realise what I'd been missing for years.

* * *

A few days later, around eight in the morning, Carlotta jumped out of bed, cursed the clock and told me she had to be in MacIntyre by nine to pick up a delivery from the Telemass station. I offered to drive her, but she said she didn't want to impose on me. She suggested we meet for drinks and dinner at the Jackeral around six, kissed me and hurried from the villa.

I dressed and made my way home, showered then sat on the balcony of the *Mantis* and ate a leisurely breakfast. I was, to tell the truth, still in a daze, and looked back over recent events as if they were a dream.

I went for a long walk after breakfast, anticipating six o'clock when we would be together again. I could not stop thinking about the woman, and wondered what the future might hold. I found myself considering the film about her ex-lover, Ed Grainger, and I wondered how Carlotta had been portrayed in Starship Fall. On impulse I downloaded the movie from the Net and sat back on the chesterfield with a beer.

The trailer promised an enthralling story of alien adventure, love and tragedy, which was pretty much the tale Carlota had told last night.

The first third of the film was an adventure story set on the movie-maker's impression of Chalcedony, an exoticised vision of alien fauna and purple mountains I would never have recognised as the real thing. Grainger was portrayed as a monomaniacal adventurer who would stop at nothing to get what he wanted. Carlotta was referred to in the first part of the film through the device of Grainger sending voice-messages to her while in space, and gazing longingly at a moving cube image of his dusky-skinned lover, played by an Indian actress.

The story had Grainger meet the aliens, only to become hooked on the bone-smoking ritual, the need to see the future. The film portrayed intrigue between the human and inimical elements of the Ashentay – and even a brief interlude of romantic interest with a native girl, which I assumed was the director's invention. Another fabrication, I guessed – at least, Carlotta had never alluded to it – was that he stole from the Ashentay a small statue of immense religious significance to the aliens, which he intended to sell in order to subsidise his ongoing explorations. He also appropriated a cache of the alien drug, to satisfy his craving.

The second third of the film was set on Earth, and documented his love for Carlotta interspersed with psychotic episodes. Carlotta came over as nothing more than a love-sick beauty, there merely to provide token romantic and sexual interest. A more sophisticated aspect of the film was the portrayal of his drug-induced visions of the future, which left the viewer guessing which one might come to pass.

In the end, against Carlotta's tearful protestations, Grainger sailed his ship back to Chalcedony, and in this version of events he rendezvoused with the religious elders in the sacred cavern. In a twist, it was revealed that he didn't sell the religious statuette as he'd intended, but returned with it as a gift for the Ashentay. In the finale, he partook one final time in the smoking of the bones, and the film closes with alternative endings – two very different visions of the future. The first had him succumbing to an overdose of the alien drug, while in the second he was reunited with Carlotta.

All in all, Carlotta's assessment of the film as a trite and sentimental was pretty much spot on, and more frustratingly from my point of view it told me nothing about Carlotta herself. Perhaps I was naïve to have hoped it might, but the fact was that I wanted to know more about the woman who, despite myself, I was falling for... or perhaps I was doing no more than falling for the glamorous image of the woman she presented to the world.

I was staring at the end credits when a chime announced that I had a visitor. I wondered if it might be Carlotta, and my heart began a laboured pounding. I turned off the screen – not wanting her to see that I had been watching the film, for fear that she might accuse me of prying into her past... which was ridiculous, I know.

I hurried from the lounge, took the drop-shaft to the entrance and hit the control to open the sliding door.

It was not Carlotta standing on the threshold, I saw with disappointment, but Kee.

71

And only then did I recall what she'd said as we parted a few days ago, and my curiosity was rekindled.

"Kee, well... this is a surprise. Why don't you come in?"

She smiled timidly and hurried past me. She wore only a sand-coloured shift, and was barefoot, her arms and legs covered with fine golden hair. We rode the elevator together, but she didn't meet my gaze.

For all that I'd known Kee for five years, and come to like her a lot, she always struck me as being intimidated by my presence; her body language and mannerisms were reserved, shy... though I know I should not ascribe human attributes to an alien people.

We entered the lounge and she sat on her favourite seat by the viewscreen which overlooked the bay. She'd made the seat her own on her many visits with Hawk, Matt and Maddie, and would stare out at the view for ages on end while we drank and chatted away.

"Can I get you something to drink, Kee?"

"A sava juice would be nice, thank you, David."

I fixed two cold juices and sat opposite Kee. "It's nice to see you," I said, somewhat uneasily. "You gave us a bit of a fright the other day, I can tell you."

Her large-eyed, thin-lipped alien face turned my way, and I wondered what was going on behind those piercingly azure eyes.

I cleared my throat. "You said you needed to see me about something." I took a sip of juice.

She inclined her head. She employed human gestures tentatively, uncertainly, much as a stranger to the English language might use unfamiliar words.

She said, "The other day I saw the future. Or rather I saw what might be the future, or rather possible futures. Who knows which future might happen in this reality?"

She fell silent.

"And?" I prompted.

72

"And the difficulty is in knowing which future might happen. Our elders have a theory, perhaps you have heard of this theory? It is that all the futures we see when we smoke the bones will come to happen, in many different realities. Our elders say that we can make the future we want in *our* reality, through guiding events to the desired outcome, and by being virtuous and good."

I smiled. "Our scientists have a theory that there are a multiplicity of differing words, an infinity of realities," I told her.

She lifted a hand in an odd gesture, much as a puppet might perform the movement. "I saw three futures, David. Two were vague, while one was more… vivid. According to our elders, the more vivid the vision, the more likely it is to happen in our reality."

"That makes sense," I murmured. I hesitated, then said, "And what were these visions?" I stopped myself, and made a performance of hitting my forehead with the palm of my hand. "Sorry. I forgot. You can't talk about them, can you?"

She smiled at my play-acting, appreciating the humour. "What I said the other day, about not being able to talk about them… I said that because Hawk was there."

I felt a sudden apprehension. "I don't see…" I began, though I did see, dimly.

She went on, "I can talk about what I saw, but I do not want to tell Hawk about what I saw. So, please, do not say anything to him. Do you promise?"

"Of course," I said. "What is it, Kee?"

"I smoked the bones, David, and then I passed out. I experienced… oh, words cannot describe the wonderful feeling. It was bliss, it was… a word Hawk sometimes uses… eu- eu…"

"Euphoric?" I suggested.

She nodded. "Yes, euphoric. I was in a different place, and I was gloriously happy. And then the visions began." She looked down at her hands, her fingers twisting.

"What did you see?"

She looked up, staring at me with massive eyes. She seemed frightened. "I saw Hawk. He was in the sacred cavern. You were there, and a tall woman with dark hair. I saw Hawk, standing beside the entrance to the chamber, and he was shouting at someone, and arguing..."

She stopped there, shaking her head from side to side as if in disbelief.

"What happened?" I prompted.

"And then... then Hawk was attacked. I think he was stabbed. He fell, holding his chest." She was crying now, hunched and weeping. She shook her head. "Then the vision changed. I saw myself alone, and weeping."

"Who attacked him?" I asked.

She shook her head. "The image was vague. I could not make out his attacker..."

I nodded, aware that my throat was dry. I told myself that what Kee had told me was no more than alien superstition, utter nonsense that had no rational bearing on how events in this world would play themselves out. I said, "And the other visions?"

She lifted her shoulders in a quick shrug. "In the other visions I saw me and Hawk, on an alien world, walking hand in hand beside a silver sea... and another vision showed me in old age, with Hawk looking after me..."

I gestured. "Well, there you are, then. Two of the three showed a happy outcome."

She screwed her pretty face into a mask of anguish. "But the first vision, the strongest vision, showed Hawk dying. This means... this means that this is more likely to happen, unless we work hard so that it will not."

I nodded, playing along with her. "And how do we do that?"

She said, "You must tell our friends, Matt and Maddie, tell them what I saw, tell them that Hawk must never again visit the scared cavern, yes?"

I nodded seriously. "Of course I'll do that."

"You see, if he does not go to the cavern, then he cannot be stabbed, can he? He will live, and I will be happy with him beside the silver alien sea, and we will live to old age together, which is what I want more than anything in the world."

"I'll go and see Matt and Maddie," I promised. "I'll tell them what you saw, okay?"

She smiled with relief. "But you must not tell Hawk that I have been to see you, David. Do not tell him about the vision, yes?"

"I won't say a word to him, Kee."

She smiled, and the expression lighted her face. "Thank you, David. I knew I could trust you."

She finished her sava juice and looked down at the glass. "I feel better now. I will go back to the yard. Hawk is working on one of his ships, as usual." She stood up.

"I'll show you out," I said, leading the way from the lounge to the drop-chute. We crossed the foyer and I slapped the sensor panel to open the sliding hatch, and Kee turned to me, stood on tip-toe and kissed my cheek.

"Goodbye, David," she said, and turned.

She stopped dead, as if yanked back on puppet strings, and stared at my approaching visitor with wide eyes.

Carlotta stood before the ship, adopting an expression of superior amusement. Kee moved around Carlotta, watching her intently, then hurried away around the ship and out of sight.

And I suddenly recalled what she'd told me, minutes ago: *You were there, and a tall woman with dark hair.*

Carlotta turned to me and raised an expressive eye-brow. "And who's your little girlfriend, David?"

I smiled, hiding my confusion. "That's Kee, Hawk's girlfriend. You know – Hawk, the pilot."

"She seemed... shocked to see me, David?"

I shrugged. "She's an odd creature," I temporised. "She's often uneasy around humans."

"But not around you, I see."

I decided to tell her the reason for her visit, omitting mention of the tall, dark woman.

"Kee underwent the bone-smoking ritual last week," I said. "And me and a few friends followed her, hoping to find her before it began. Look, why don't you come inside and I'll tell you all about it."

She nodded. "You didn't mention this before, David."

I led her into the ship and to the lounge. I poured her a sava juice and sat beside her on the chesterfield. "I've had other things on my mind, Carlotta," I said. "Hey, you've stopped calling me Conway."

She reached out and stroked my cheek. We kissed. She said, "Tell me about the sacred cavern."

So I gave her the story, doing my best to describe the cavern, the aliens, and the strange ritual, or rather as much of it as we'd witnessed. She hung on my words, and I could see that she was imagining her ex-lover, the pilot Grainger, going through the same ritual.

"But why did the girl come to see you?" Carlotta asked. She opened her mouth in a silent, "Ah..." then went on, "It was about what she saw, yes?"

I nodded, and described what Kee had told me, editing the 'dark woman' from the account. I knew, rationally, that this could not refer to Carlotta, but even so I thought it best not to confuse the issue by mentioning it.

"And she said that Hawk's death was the strongest image?"

"She did. Not that I hold much credence in it—"

Carlotta was looking at me oddly. "We scoff at mysteries we do not understand at our own expense, David. From what I know of the drug... well, there's something in it."

I stared at her. "You're serious, aren't you?"

She nodded. "There were times, after Ed had smoked drug, when he'd make a decision that would turn out to be spectacularly correct."

I laughed. "Intuition," I said. "He had a drug-induced vision, believed in it so much that his strength of will brought about the desired result."

She tipped her head, her lips screwed to one side in a *maybe* gesture. "Or perhaps the drug did grant him a foretaste of the future."

I hesitated, then said, "When you smoked the stuff... you believed what you saw?"

"I told you what I saw – myself, alone... and it was enough to make me believe, and to beg Ed not to go..."

I smiled and shrugged. "Anyway, to be on the safe side we'll make sure that Hawk doesn't visit the sacred cavern in a hurry."

She nodded seriously. "I'd do that, David. Now," she said, with a lascivious smile, "I thought that kiss earlier was going to lead to something more."

"I think perhaps it might," I said.

* * *

Carlotta left a while later, arranging to meet me at the Jackeral that evening, and I realised that I'd never got round to asking what she'd picked up from the Telemass station that afternoon. I showered, dressed, and decided to visit Matt and Maddie and tell them about Kee's visit.

I was about to leave the *Mantis* when the com chimed.

I accepted the call and the screen showed Maddie, grinning out at me. "What a coincidence," I said. "I was just about to come   over."

"Do that, you old dog, and tell us all about it."

"What?" I said, all innocent.

She laughed and said over her shoulder to Matt, "He says 'what?', as if butter wouldn't melt in his mouth."

"Word travels fast," I laughed.

"Old Ben Henderson and his cronies saw you two leaving the Jackeral hot foot the other night," she said. "And since then you've been inseparable. His crowd don't miss much."

"Anyway, I wasn't coming over to tell you about me and Carlotta, Maddie. Sorry to disappoint you. But I had Kee here this afternoon. She was in a bit of a state."

She looked alarmed. "Is Hawk okay?"

"He's fine. Look, I'll be over to tell you all about it. Get the beer chilled."

I cut the connection and hurried from the ship.

I made my way around the bay to Matt and Maddie's dome. The sun was high and hot, and by the time I arrived thirty minutes later I'd worked up a fair thirst.

They were sitting on the verandah overlooking the bay, and waved as I trudged up the sand. I climbed the steps and joined them, and Matt dutifully poured me an ice cold beer.

Maddie said, "You'll be needing this, David."

Deadpan, I said, "Yes, it's a fair walk."

"I wasn't referring to the walk," she said, touching a pair of binoculars on the table before her.

"I don't believe it!" I appealed to Matt. "Does this woman have no shame? Spying on friends, now?"

Matt shrugged. "I don't know what to do with her," he said.

Maddie said, "So... you think this is the real thing, David?"

Before I could reply, Matt said, "We always think it's the real thing, don't we?" He stared out to sea. "That's the beauty and the wonder of it, and sometimes the tragedy."

Maddie laughed. "Listen to the philosopher!"

Matt hoisted his glass and smiled.

Maddie was still looking at me, eyebrow raised.

I said, "I... it's early days. Who can tell? But it's certainly intense."

She reached out and squeezed my hand. "Good for you, David."

Matt hoisted his beer. "To the happy couple."

I took a long drink and licked froth from my upper lip. "About Kee... I don't know, but it's eerie..."

"Tell," Maddie commanded.

I recounted Kee's visit, her description of the visions. "She said she saw Hawk attacked and stabbed. She said he was in the chamber with me and a tall, dark haired woman when it happened."

Maddie frowned. "Anyone she knew?"

"That's just it. As Kee was leaving, Carlotta was paying me a visit – as you well know," I said. "And Kee's expression when she saw Carlotta... it was as if she'd seen a ghost."

Maddie shrugged. "It might not necessarily mean that Carlotta and the woman in Kee's vision were the same."

"Well, it might not. But it struck me that Kee thought so. Anyway, she wanted me to come and tell you. We have to keep Hawk from the sacred cavern, at all costs."

Matt said, "That shouldn't be too difficult."

Maddie was watching me. "What do you think about it... the ritual, this vision business?"

I shrugged. "Well, the rationalist in me thinks it's bunkum. But that tiny part of me, the superstitious heathen in my hind-brain..."

"I know what you mean, David. Look at it from the Ashentay's point of view. They're conditioned to believe, and if they have visions which they *do* believe in strongly enough, then maybe the power of suggestion is so powerful that it might bring about the envisioned events. A kind of self-fulfilling prophecy."

"That's about where I stand on it," I said. "But if Hawk did get stabbed in the sacred cavern..." I shrugged. "If that did happen, then I'd become a convert."

Maddie said, "Presumably Hawk doesn't know anything about this?"

"That's right. Kee asked us not to breathe a word."

"Poor girl. She must be in a terrible state."

"Well, she doesn't believe that what she saw was written in stone," I said. "Her people believe that the visions don't necessarily come to pass, that things can be done to circumvent them." I shrugged. "The sight of Carlotta shook her, though."

"Spooky." Maddie shivered. "Another beer?"

We drank as the afternoon progressed, the conversation moving onto other things, and eventually back – perhaps inevitably – to my liaison with Carlotta.

Maddie said, "But you won't leave us if she decides Magenta is too much of a backwater, will you, David?"

"Lay off!" I protested good-naturedly.

"Why don't you stay for something to eat?" Matt asked. "We were thinking of having a barbecue. Henderson gave us a flat-head he caught earlier."

Maddie laughed. "Don't be so silly, Matt! David has other fish to fry."

"At the Jackeral," I said, groaning at her pun and examining my watch, "in under one hour. I'd better be off."

"Tell us all about it the next time we meet!" Maddie called as I made my way from the verandah.

I smiled and waved and, as I wandered back through the scented pines, I thought how lucky I was to have such great friends… and now Carlotta.

I arrived back at the *Mantis*, dressed for dinner, and arrived at the Jackeral with ten minutes to spare.

* * *

Carlotta breezed in on the stroke of seven. Heads turned as she made her way to the bar, stunning in a yellow, off-the-shoulder dress with a flower of the same colour pinned in her hair. The dress complemented her mocha skin, and as if to emphasise the Indian in her she wore a crimson tikka-spot on her forehead.

She pecked my cheek in greeting and whispered, "Great to see you, David," and I thought I was going to have a heart attack.

"Shall we have a drink at the bar, and then dine?" she said, sliding onto the bar-stool beside mine. "I'll have the usual."

I ordered another beer and a vodka and sava for Carlotta, and I asked her how her day in MacIntyre had gone.

"It was a success. I collected what I went for and miraculously it had survived the Telemass journey intact."

"What was it?"

"It's a secret, David. But I'll show you later tonight, hm? That is, if you want to come back to my place?"

I smiled. "Try keeping me away," I said, my curiosity piqued.

We drank and chatted and I felt totally relaxed in her company. The David Conway of just one week ago, had he been able to look ahead and see himself in the presence of this beautiful woman, would have been amazed; looking back, I had assumed I was happy then, but what I felt now was close to euphoria.

We had another drink and then moved to the dining area; I had grilled jackeral and Carlotta a local salad, and as we ate she regaled me with hilarious stories of the great and the good – and the not so great and good – she had met during her time as a world-famous holo star.

She laughed a lot, and touched me, and I compared her present mood to how unhappy she had been just days ago, and I marvelled that I had made such a difference.

I told her about my life in British Columbia, and she asked about my wife. I told her that the marriage had been happy, but that it had no way of surviving the death of my daughter.

She quickly touched my hand. "Don't, David. I can see it still hurts. Tell me about the *Mantis* instead. I've seen the film, but I want the truth."

So I told her how I'd bought the *Mantis* from Hawk's junkyard, and how just days later I'd seen the first alien ghost

81

aboard it… and how, a while later, the ghost of the Yall had led us to the miracle of the golden column.

"And to think," Carlotta declared, at her most thespian, "I am intimate with the Opener of the Way!"

We laughed and drank and, come midnight, we were happily sozzled.

"And now," she said, standing and swaying and pulling me up from the table. "Now I want to show you something. Back to my place, my man."

I allowed myself to be taken, and we slogged through the magenta sands which scintillated in the Ringlight, almost falling once or twice and laughing at our clumsiness.

At last we made it to her villa.

"Sit right there," she said, pushing me into the sofa and swaying over me. "Don't move, and I'll show you… I'll show you an invaluable work of art."

I opened my mouth to ask what it was, but she shushed me with a long finger pressed to the crimson slash of her mouth, and tottered into the next room.

She returned a minute later carrying a box perhaps half a metre square. She placed it with exaggerated care on a small coffee table, then knelt on the carpet, reached out and touched something on the side of the box.

The sides unfolded as if by magic, revealing a small carved figure standing on a plinth.

I gasped. It was the religious relic which, in the film Starship Fall, Ed Grainger had taken from the sacred cavern.

"So that part of the film was true to life?" I began

She blinked at me. "You've seen it all the way through?"

I told her about the download. "But in the film," I said, "Grainger returned here with it…" I shook my head. "But obviously not in reality."

Carlotta stared at the carving, her eyes massive. She said, "What really happened, David, is that Ed sold the relic to finance his explorations. It went into the xenological museum in Paris. He tried to get it back when he decided to return here, but they weren't giving it up that easily – and he didn't have the cash they were asking for it."

"So how come..." I said, gesturing at the statue.

"I made them an offer they couldn't refuse, and for the past few weeks I've been waiting for the relevant authorities in Europe to sanction its release."

"And now," I said, "you can return it to the Ashentay as Ed would have wished?"

She smiled. "Closure, David..." She paused, then went on, "But I also want something from them, you see. It came to me that if I returned the relic, then they might help me locate where Ed's ship landed, or crash-landed."

I nodded, feeling adolescent jealousy despite myself.

Then I said, before I knew I was saying it, "I could help you, Carlotta. I mean, I know the way to Dar, the Ashentay village not far from the sacred cavern. I even know someone who could guide us the rest of the way."

Her face illuminated. "David, you don't know how much... Come here." She reached out and took me in a passionate embrace, and seconds later she was sobbing against my shoulder.

"It's been so long, David. So long, and I finally want an end to the... the grief. I want closure."

"And then?" I asked.

She answered me, between kisses. "And." Kiss. "Then." Kiss. "Who knows what the future." Kiss. "Holds?"

She dragged me to the bedroom, and all I could concentrate on was the glorious present.

* * *

In the morning, as the sun climbed and filled the bedroom with its golden light, we held each other and I suggested that later we drive down to MacIntyre and hire a bison.

I left her villa, arranging to pick her up in an hour, and hurried over to the *Mantis*. I showered and changed, and was about to dash out when the com chimed. I had half a mind to ignore it, but on impulse accepted the call.

Kee's innocent child's face filled the screen. She was leaning close, staring intently. "David!"

"Kee, what is it?"

"David, the woman I saw yesterday. She was the same woman I saw in my vision of the scared cavern!"

I shook my head. "Are you sure...?"

"David – please tell me. Are you going to the cavern?"

I blinked. "Ah..."

"David! Please – don't go!"

"Kee, Kee, calm down. There's no need to worry. Trust me. We're merely going to return something that belongs to your people."

She interrupted, "But the woman, David! I saw her in my—" She stopped suddenly and glanced, frightened, over her shoulder. Then I heard Hawk's muffled enquiry, "What woman, Kee? Who are you talking to?"

"No one!" she almost screamed.

"Kee," Hawk said, and I saw his torso behind her as he moved towards the screen.

"No," Kee cried, and cut the connection.

I stood there for ten seconds, in a daze of indecision, wondering whether to call Hawk and explain the situation. In the end, not wanting to alert him to Kee's vision, I thought it best to leave well alone.

I hurried from the dome and collected Carlotta and the boxed relic, and we drove south to MacIntyre in the glorious autumn sunlight.

One hour later, after hiring a bison and setting off inland, a combination of Carlotta's exhilarating company and my rationalism persuaded me that Kee's outburst had been nothing more than heightened alien superstition. I told myself that Carlotta might have born a passing resemblance to a woman in Kee's drug-induced dream, but the idea that Kee had been granted a glimpse into the future was ridiculous.

"What are you thinking about, David?" Carlotta asked, resting her head against the back of the seat and gazing at me with loving eyes.

I smiled. "I was just thinking about how happy I am," I said.

Nine

We reached Dar just after midday. If the Ashentay were surprised at the appearance of a second set of humans within a week, they gave no sign. A posse of tiny children crowded the bison as I braked on the outskirts of the village. We climbed down and approached the few adults who had bothered to emerge from their huts at the sound of the vehicle's engine.

The emaciated elder, Jyrik, faced us and spoke in his language. I was about to gesture, helplessly, that I could not understand.

Then, to my astonishment, Carlotta stepped froward and spoke in halting Ashentay.

I stared at her when she'd finished. She smiled. "Not just a pretty face, David. I've been teaching myself the language for months."

The elder replied, and seconds later the slim, lithe guide called Qah appeared at his side.

Carlotta inclined her head and spoke her thanks.

We returned to the bison and I gunned the engine, heading away from the village towards the flattened jungle where the first bison had broadened the path. Qah sat behind us, leaning through the gap in the front seats and speaking to Carlotta. When Carlotta failed to reply, or spoke only the occasional monosyllable, Qah gave up.

I glanced at Carlotta. She seemed withdrawn now that we were so close to the sacred cavern, almost nervous. She leaned forward, staring ahead at the tangled undergrowth, and I wondered if she were thinking back to the time her lover Ed

Grainger had found himself in the jungle of Chalcedony... Jealousy burned in my gut like bile.

I said, to provoke a response from her, "We drove the bison for a couple of hours last time, Carlotta. When we couldn't go any further, we walked the rest of the way. That took about another two hours."

I glanced at her, but she only nodded minimally.

"I must say it was hard going, in the humidity and all..."

"Yes," she said abstractedly, "I guess it must have been."

I turned my attention to forcing the bison over the uneven terrain. The fact that we were following the track originally laid down by the first bison made the job a little easier, but I was no expert at off-road driving. We stalled often and once, stupidly, I even found I'd taken a wrong turning. Qah soon put me right, calling out in her breathy language and pointing out the correct way.

Three hours later the bison stalled again, butting up against the fallen tree trunk that had impeded the first bison. Qah said something to Carlotta.

"This is the end of the road. We walk from here."

We climbed from the cab and I shouldered my rucksack, which contained food and water. In Carlotta's was the religious relic, well packed. Qah skipped off like a gazelle and we did our best to follow. Thankfully, Carlotta was dressed for the occasion in slacks, blouse and sturdy boots. If anything, the casual, androgynous apparel emphasised her glamour. She looked like the female lead in some low-budget jungle adventure holo.

I found the trek just as hard going this time around. To my surprise – call it overweening male pride, if you will – Carlotta forged ahead in Qah's wake, and they had to stop from time to time and wait for me to catch them up. I was relieved to see that Carlotta didn't resent the delay I was causing; she had her water canister awaiting me, and even kissed my forehead with a tolerant smile.

A couple of hours later we came to the clearing before the waterfall, and Carlotta stopped and stood, legs planted astride, fists on hips: against the silver fall of water she cut a magnificent figure.

"I never thought I'd see the day..." she began, clearly overcome.

She turned to Qah and spoke Ashentay.

The girl replied.

"What?" I asked.

Carlotta said, "I told her I had something, a gift for the elder in the sacred cavern." So saying, she unshouldered her rucksack and carefully eased out the wrapped statuette. She pulled off the foam packing, and Qah just stared with massive eyes. She said something, and reached out to touch the figure.

Then she looked at Carlotta, made a quick hand gesture and hurried off across the clearing. Seconds later she vanished behind the sheer waterfall.

Carlotta returned the relic to her rucksack, then strode off a little way, staring into the distance. I sensed that she wanted some time alone to contemplate the past, and the immediate future.

Selfishly, I looked ahead to when she had accomplished what she had come here to do, when she could close the book on this chapter of her life and look ahead.

I sat beside my rucksack, took out the water and drank while admiring the spectacular view, the jungle-cloaked mountains and the Ring of Tharssos arcing overhead. The scene was so exquisitely alien that my human emotions – my feelings for Carlotta, and my jealousy – seemed puny by comparison, insignificant and unworthy of the setting.

When I next glanced at Carlotta, I saw that she had removed herself even further from me and was smoking a cigarette. I found this surprising, as she'd never smoked before in my presence. The fool in me ascribed it to nerves – and then I caught of whiff of the smoke on the warm breeze.

In retrospect, I think she wanted me to learn the truth so that I might find more acceptable what she had to tell me.

She turned to me and stared.

I stood. "Carlotta...?"

I approached her, warily. I gestured, lamely, at the half-smoked cigarette. "The drug," I murmured.

She smiled, almost sadly, and nodded.

I could only say, "But I thought..." I began. "I thought Grainger used up all his supply."

"I took a little more than I originally told you, David. Not much, but now—"

My heart fluttered. "I don't understand," I said, and I meant it. I was confused, and a little frightened. I recalled her avowal that she had used the drug but twice: she had lied to me, and if she had lied once...

How much of our relationship, I asked myself, was founded on lies?

"Carlotta?" I almost pleaded.

"David," she said in a reasonable tone, "you must understand what it's like, to see the future, or what might be the future, to be granted a glimpse... It – it becomes addictive, not biologically, but psychologically. Just one more hit, you say, hoping that the next time the visions will be that much clearer, easier to interpret. So you do it again, and again, and again... and by that time you're habituated, and you can't stop."

"You could have told me," I said.

She shook her head. "I... I didn't want you to think that my attraction to you might have been my merely following some predestination laid down in a vision."

That rocked me. I felt a strange heat rise up my chest and engulf my head. "And was it?" I managed.

"I... I don't think so, David. I looked into the future, and I saw us together, but what I felt when I met you... what I feel for you now... that can't be denied, David."

I said, "The drug. The relic. All this is about getting at the real drug, isn't it?"

She hesitated, looking at me. I thought I saw calculation on her massive Indian eyes, and I understood only later what she was in fact calculating. She said, "I want to see the future even more clearly," she murmured.

I wanted to ask her, "And then? When will it stop?" but I resisted the impulse. I thought back to my very first meeting with Carlotta Chakravorti-Luna, and I realised that she'd artfully arranged it, set up the tableau outside the *Mantis* as carefully as any pre-scripted holo-movie…

And I felt sick.

Before I might react, break down and yell at her, accuse her of lies and deceit, Qah emerged from behind the waterfall and ran across to us. She spoke to Carlotta, who turned to me.

"I'm going, David. You can stay here if you want, or if you'd rather come with me…"

I wanted to be strong enough to turn away and walk off, but the truth was that I cared for Carlotta too much to leave her to her fate.

She turned and followed Qah into the caverns, and I hurried after them.

We descended, Carlotta and Qah moving swiftly ahead of me while I, exhausted from the trek so far, failed to keep up. By the time I arrived at the cavern, Carlotta had reached the long-house and paused, something in her poise almost reminiscent of a worshipper at the altar of a cathedral. The tall elder, hidden behind his ornate face-mask, stood in the entrance of the long-house and stared down at her.

Slowly, Carlotta unwrapped the relic and held it up to the elder in both hands. He nodded, once, gravely, and she spoke to him.

I arrived behind her, and stopped. Qah was staring at Carlotta, her eyes wide, and beside her were the four Ashentay bearers, staring also.

Slowly Carlotta turned to me. A look of infinite pity filled her eyes as she said, "David, I must do this. I hope you understand. I... I must learn where my destiny lies..."

"Carlotta," I said. "We could be so..." but I could say no more.

She smiled and said, "Thank you, David," and turned and walked up the ramp towards the elder. She paused before him, and they looked at each other for what seemed like an age, and then he inclined his masked head and she passed into the shadow of the long-house. The elder gazed down at me, then turned and followed.

I felt a hand on my shoulder. Qah. She gestured to a seat – a shelf recessed into the wall of the cavern and padded with grass – and I crossed to the wall and slumped down.

* * *

I must have slept. I was startled a while later by the chime of my wrist-com. I sat up, fumbled with the device and stared at the tiny screen.

Maddie frowned out at me. "David, I thought you'd never answer! Are you in the cavern?" The picture sizzled, broke up. The reception was bad, this far underground.

"Yes," I answered, confused. "What's wrong?"

"We're on our way–" She went on, but static masked her words.

"Maddie?"

"Kee contacted us... explained what was happening. She was distraught. Apparently Hawk overheard her talking to you. When he found out that Carlotta was going to the cavern with you... he told Kee that he had to follow her. He told her that he suspected something–"

"*Suspected?*" I said.

92

"Kee didn't say what."

I shook my head. "I don't see..." I began, befuddled by the surreal exchange.

"I don't understand either," Maddie said. "Anyway, Hawk's heading your way in a bison. We're following with Kee." She stared out at me. "Where's Carlotta?"

I told her.

"Oh, Christ, David. Listen, we'll soon be with you–" The picture broke up and Maddie vanished. I tried to return the call, but to no avail.

I lay down, staring at the roof of the cavern, at the dancing shadows cast by the bonfires. I thought through what had happened so far, what was happening now – and the fact that Hawk was making his way here. I considered what Kee had told me, and my rationality reeled.

Later, perhaps an hour later, a combination of exhaustion and the heat down there conspired to send me to sleep, and I have no idea how long I was out... Hours, at least, for I awoke to see Hawk striding into the sacred cavern followed by a host of concerned Ashentay, like children milling at the legs of a giant.

He stood just in side the threshold and stared at the long-house.

I stumbled to my feet and waved at him.

He glanced across the chamber at me, then back to the long-house. His expression was an odd combination of fear and awe, and only later did I come to understand why.

I rubbed my eyes and stumbled towards him; he strode past me, intent on the long-house. He was muttering something under his breath, like a man deranged, and I thought I caught, "Surely... surely not, after so long?"

He stopped at the foot of the ramp, staring up, and called out, "Is it really you in there?"

Blood pounded in my head, misting my vision. I stared at the long-house and saw the tall figure of the elder emerge. He stood at the top of the ramp, staring down at Hawk.

"Hawksworth," said the being behind the mask.

"You were always one for the grand gesture," Hawk said, "the theatrics. Well, you've had your time—"

The elder reached up and removed the ornate face-mask that covered his head, and I saw that he was not an Ashentay at all, but a human, a balding, long-faced man in his late fifties.

He stared down at Hawk with bright blue eyes and said, "I've found my place at last, Hawksworth. I know where I belong."

Hawk sneered. "A bolt hole, a hiding place."

"No, Hawksworth," Grainger said with what seemed like infinite patience, "my rightful place in the universe, providing a service to a wise race."

"That's all over, Grainger, You've had your period of reprieve. I've come for you…"

Grainger laughed. "Hawksworth, listen to me. You fail. You don't leave here with me. I know. You see, I've seen how things work out, I've looked upon my destiny."

"Your destiny," Hawk said, "is that you're going to pay for what you did to me back then…" He stopped as Grainger stepped forward and came down the ramp. I thought at first that, despite his fine words, Grainger was about to give himself up. I should have known, though; I should have recalled what Kee had said she had seen in her vision, but the truth was that Kee's warning was the last thing on my mind as I watched the drama unfold.

Grainger came to the foot of the ramp and faced Hawk, two big men confronting each other as everyone else, the stretcher-bearers and the other Ashentay and myself, looked on. Then Hawk moved, as if to reach out and take Grainger's arm – and Grainger's reaction was lightning fast. In a swift underarm gesture he stabbed his ceremonial spear up and into Hawk's midriff. Even across the cavern I heard the bloody squelch as the blade tore through muscle. Hawk stared down as if in disbelief at the shaft protruding from his diaphragm, then fell to his knees.

The Ashentay moved; they surrounded Grainger and bundled him away, unprotesting, to whatever justice the aliens meted out for such crimes, and I ran to Hawk and held him. The spear had lanced through his stomach and ripped through his back; I judged that it had missed his spine by a fraction, and this was confirmed when Hawk gasped, "David, help me to my feet..."

I held him, eased him up, and took his weight. Blood spread across the front of his jacket, which acted as a sponge. I looped an arm around his back and attempted to half-carry him from the cavern. I felt the thick syrupy ooze of it across my forearm. His breath came in spasms, and from time to time he cried out in pain.

We stumbled through the narrow tunnel, just wide enough to allow me to remain by Hawk's side, holding him and urging him on. I was exhausted, and Hawk had lost God knows how much blood, and I could only imagine the pain he was obviously suffering – but he was a strong man and he dragged himself up the chiselled steps with a fierce determination, as if to defy Grainger's best attempts to kill him, and Kee's terrible foretelling of the future.

I was too taken up by the events of the moment to consider Kee's vision and what this might mean. Only later, in the long days back in Magenta Bay, could I reflect on all that had happened and ponder the philosophical implications of Hawk's succumbing to his lover's prophecy.

Ten minutes later we emerged from behind the waterfall into blazing sunlight. Delta Pavonis was lifting itself over the mountains, and I realised that I had spent all night and much of the morning deep underground.

My plan was to take Hawk back through the jungle to the bison, which was equipped with emergency medical supplies –

but in the event, thankfully, I was saved that gruelling journey.

I heard a sudden scream, and looked up to see Kee sprinting across the clearing, closely followed by Matt and Maddie. Kee was carrying something – a medi-kit, I realised: forewarned by her vision – and her face as she stared at Hawk, at the monstrous weapon that skewered him, was a mask of anguish.

Hawk fell to his knees. Matt was already tearing open the medi-case and withdrawing a hypoject of painkiller. He pumped it into Hawk's thigh, followed by an coagulant, then eased Hawk onto his side on the grass.

Maddie was a few metres away, speaking urgently into her wrist-com. She returned to us. "I've alerted the air-medics in MacIntyre. They'll be here within the hour."

Kee sat beside Hawk and gripped his hand and sobbed as he lapsed in an out of consciousness. "I'm sorry, Hawk," she murmured. "I'm so sorry!"

At least, I saw, the wound had ceased bleeding. I looked enquiringly at Matt, who said, "I don't know. Touch and go. Hawk's a tough old bastard. If anyone can make it..."

Maddie said, "Carlotta...?"

I shook my head. "She... she entered the long-house," was all I could bring myself to say.

Maddie held my hand. "David, there's nothing you can do here. Go back to her, be there when she comes out, okay?"

"Are you sure?"

I was torn between waiting until the medics had assessed Hawk, and being there when Carlotta emerged from the long-house so that I could question her... I had so much I wanted to ask.

I nodded. "I'll go." I glanced at Hawk. He was unconscious, which eased my guilt at fleeing.

I hurried back to the waterfall and made the long descent. Here and there I saw slicks of Hawk's spilled blood, black in the pale fungal light.

I came to the sacred cavern; only the stretcher-bearers were apparent, sitting off to one side of the long-house. A part of me expected to see Carlotta there, dazed after her session with the alien drug. I wondered, then, at how I might receive her, and her me.

The future was uncertain. I knew what I felt for the woman, but I feared learning that she felt nothing at all for me. More than anything I wanted to know if she had used me as no more than a puppet on the strings of pre-destination, if her apparent love for me had been no more than an act.

I sat cross-legged at the foot of the ramp, hung my head and waited. An age seemed to elapse. I drifted, catching myself with a start again and again as I almost fell asleep. I looked ahead, and saw Carlotta and myself together and happy in Magenta Bay, and I looked ahead and saw myself alone... I told myself that some residual smoke of the burning bones was seeping from the long-house, imbuing me with diluted visions of possible futures, but the fact was my fevered mind was producing these scenarios without the aid of any alien stimulant.

I looked up. There was movement in the entrance of the long-house. An elder, Grainger's replacement, a slight figure upon whom the face-mask seemed disproportionately large, appeared on the threshold, then stood to one side and thumped his spear.

From nowhere Qah appeared at my side, and touched my shoulder. I tried to read the expression in her big eyes, but could not. She gestured towards the entrance to the long-house, and I looked up. The stretcher-bearers emerged, moving with circumspection as they carried the laden stretcher down the ramp. I glimpsed a fall of midnight hair.

And I knew then that all my questions, all my doubts, would never be answered.

Ten

Two weeks later I attended the private viewing of Matt's latest art-work.

There were perhaps fifty people gathered on the red sand before his dome, standing in groups, drinking and chatting and anticipating the preview. I recognised the great and the good from Magenta and MacIntyre, and even one or two off-world critics among the crowd.

Kee stood off to one side of the group as, one by one, the effulgent spheres appeared as if by magic in the air above the sand. She was talking to Maddie, gripping a glass of sava juice and taking small sips from time to time. She looked, without Hawk by her side, smaller than usual, somehow diminished – which is a paradox because, when in Hawk's towering presence she seemed a childlike, almost a waif-like, figure.

I was on my fifth beer, and I felt mellow.

I stood and listened to a couple of speeches; a Terran critic said a few words about Matt Sommers' standing in the world of art, and then Matt stepped forward, characteristically reserved and modest, and said that his art didn't need explanation: what mattered was the experience. He went on to say that in today's world it was easy to succumb to despair; it was easy, he said, to allow one's experience of tragedy and disappointment to colour one's view of the world: the secret, he went on, was from time to time to be able to look beyond the personal...

He glanced my way as he said this, and I felt compelled to raise my beer in acknowledgement.

Then I caught sight of a tall figure emerging from behind

Matt's dome and edging towards the gathering. I liberated another beer from a passing waiter and moved towards the newcomer.

"Hawk," I said. "Great to see you. Matt'll be delighted."

I embraced him, feeling his solidity, and handed him the beer.

I'd visited him in hospital in MacIntyre, once he was well enough to see people, but we'd avoided talking about what had happened in the Ashentay's sacred cavern.

I led him towards the gathering. Kee looked up, and the light in her eyes was a delight to behold. She hurried over to him and they embraced.

A dozen spheres filled the beach, and Matt declared the preview open, and people moved towards the glowing globes, at first circumspectly, and then, having experienced one, moving with eagerness towards the next.

Kee skipped away and stepped into a sphere.

I held back and watched.

* * *

A while later Hawk fetched me a beer and we sat in the dunes overlooking the beach.

He chugged at his bottle, his movements a little stiff following the surgery to save his life.

After a period of companionable silence, I said, "What happened, Hawk, back then with Grainger?"

It was a while before he replied.

"He ran a small exploration company," he said, watching the crowd, "just after the Telemass technology made the big concerns a thing of the past. He cut corners and worked on a shoestring and made things work. I applied for work as a co-pilot. Chalcedony was the second world we explored... We came crash-landed inland a few hundred kays from here – something in the nav-system malfunctioned, and the secondaries misfired. It was a miracle we landed in one piece. Grainger was okay, but I was in a bad way. We had precious little in the way of a surgical-AI onboard, the com-rig was shot, and the ship wouldn't fly."

I shook my head. "What happened?"

"Grainger'd been here before, on a pre-exploratory trip. He said there were natives. He was going to contact them, get medical help. He set off. It was a hell of a hike... a few hundred kays to the nearest settlement." He shrugged and fell silent, his eyes distant as he looked into the past.

"Well," he went on, "when he didn't come back, I assumed he hadn't made it. I patched myself up as well as I was able, and if I'd been a believer I would have prayed."

"How did you make it back?" I asked. "I thought you said the ship wouldn't fly?"

"It wouldn't. I was rescued. A Heatherington exploration vessel was making a fly-by and picked up the ship's radiation signature. They came down to have a closer look, and the rest's history. I told them about Grainger, and they searched but found nothing. I just assumed at the time that the poor bastard had died."

I took a swallow of beer. "Was it a coincidence that you made Chalcedony your home, Hawk?"

He shook his head, smiled. "When I couldn't get work as a pilot any more, I came here, set up the junkyard, and in my spare time searched the central massifs for any sign of Grainger. I wanted to ensure that he hadn't survived, that he hadn't just walked out on me and left me for dead."

"And then, just last week, you found out."

He nodded, bitterly. "That first time in the cavern, after Kee survived... something about the elder... I wondered, but told myself not to be so ridiculous. Anyway, when I overheard Kee on the com to you, I forced her to tell me what the hell was going on. I asked myself why Carlotta might want to go to the cavern.

101

It was just too much of a coincidence, given that Carlotta and Grainger had been lovers." He stopped, then said, "I didn't believe Kee's vision, but I just knew it had to be Grainger." He shrugged. "You know the rest, David."

I stared at the floating spheres and drank my beer.

"Did you find out what the Ashentay did with Grainger?"

He nodded. "They're a peaceable people, David. They're tolerant. Kee told me that they exiled him, and deprived him of the bone drug. I... I don't know where he is. Matt made enquiries. I think he knows."

"Will you–?" I began.

Hawk smiled. "I'm not going to ask him, David. I don't want to know where the bastard is. That period of my life is over. It's enough to know that Grainger left me for dead... I don't believe in an eye for an eye. And anyway, his doing without the drug will be punishment enough."

We sat in silence for a while, as the sun sank towards the sea and the shadows lengthened. At last Hawk said, softly, "I'm sorry about Carlotta, David."

I nodded, took another swallow of beer, and said nothing.

After all, what was there to say; what could I say to explain, or excuse, her actions? I could not work out her motivations, her rationale. Had she still been in love with Ed Grainger, and used me to get to him, guided by drug-induced visions of the future? Or had she merely been a slave to the drug, and craved knowledge of her destiny, whether or not she might ever return to her exalted status as a holo superstar?

I prefer to think that what she told me, on the plain before the caverns, was the truth: *"I looked into the future, and I saw us together, but what I felt when I met you… what I feel for you now... that can't be denied, David."*

But all I do know, for certain, is that I miss Carlotta Chakravorti-Luna like hell.

Maddie emerged from the crowd and headed our way.

"David," she said, her expression compassionate as she looked down at me. She reached out, and I took her hand.

She pulled me upright. "Come," she ordered. She linked an arm through mine and squeezed.

Kee joined us, taking Hawk's hand as we walked toward the nearest floating sphere. I felt his arm about my shoulders.

They steered me towards the sphere, and then Matt himself, the creator, smiling as he joined us, took Maddie's hand.

"What's it called, Matt?" I asked, pointing towards the sphere.

He said, "I call it, *The Love of Friends*, David."

All around, the assembly had paused to watch us, and I felt a sudden tightness in my chest, the result of some unnameable emotion, part grief, part loneliness, part love.

Together we approached the light.

Eric Brown:
A Selected bibliography

Novels:
Meridian Days – *Pan Macmillan*, 1992
Engineman – *Pan Macmillan*, 1994
Penumbra – *Orion*, 1999
New York Nights – *Gollancz*, 2000
New York Blues – *Gollancz*, 2002
New York Dreams – *Gollancz*, 2004
Helix – *Solaris*, 2007
Kethani – *Solaris*, 2008
Necropath – *Solaris*, 2008
Xenopath – *Solaris*, 2009
Cosmopath – *Solaris*, 2010

Novellas:
The Web: Untouchable – *Orion Dolphin*, 1997
The Web: Walkabout – *Orion Dolphin*, 1999
A Writer's Life – *PS Publishing*, 2001
Approaching Omega – *Telos Publications*, 2005
The Extraordinary Voyage of Jules Verne – *PS Publishing*, 2005
Revenge – *Barrington Stoke*, 2007
Starship Summer – *PS Publishing*, 2007
Starship Fall – *NewCon Press*, 2009
Gilbert and Edgar on Mars – *PS Publishing*, 2009

Collections:
The Time-Lapsed Man and other stories – *Pan Macmillan*, 1990
Blue Shifting – *Pan Macmillan*, 1995
Parallax View (with Keith Brooke) – *Sarob Press*, 2000
Deep Future – *Cosmos Books*, 2001
The Fall of Tartarus – *Gollancz*, 2005
Threshold Shift – *Golden Gryphon*, 2006

New from NewCon Press

THE BELOVED OF MY BELOVED
Ian Watson & Roberto Quaglia / Roberto Quaglia & Ian Watson
British Science Fiction meets Italian Surrealism

Tattooed upon a woman-sized tumour, these tales told to it as bedtime stories are surreal, satiric, erotic, ingenious, outrageous and hilarious, forming a very weird love story unique in literature; the product of an English and an Italian brain working as one. Prepare to be shocked, prepare to be astonished, prepare to be amused and prepare to be amazed... An incredible saga; though not one for the faint-hearted.

THE GIFT OF JOY
Ian Whates

Eighteen stories, five original to this collection, which take you to distant futures and disturbing tomorrows, to strange new worlds and others that may seem uncomfortably familiar. Intelligent science fiction and telling fantasy, packed with excitement, surprises, humour, and warmth.

"Ian Whates has a way with words, a storyteller's sensibility and is rapidly developing the writing skills to match. Definitely one to watch." *Jon Courtenay Grimwood.*

"Darkly funny tales of the unexpected, with a deft science-fictional turn of the knife." *Ken MacLeod*

Also from NewCon Press:

disLOCATIONS

edited by Ian Whates

A limited edition anthology, each copy numbered and signed by all
contributors, with stories by:
**Chaz Brenchley, Pat Cadigan, Hal Duncan, Amanda
Hemingway, Andrew Hook, Ken MacLeod, Adam Roberts, Brian
Stableford, and Andy West.**

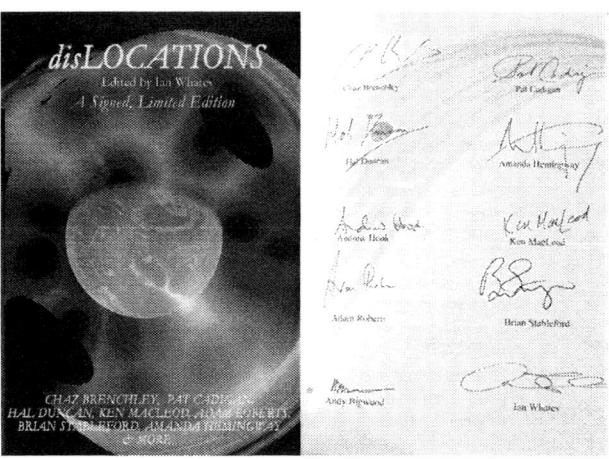

Lighting Out – Ken MacLeod   Winner, best short story, BSFA Awards
Selected for Gardner Dozois' 'Year's Best'
The Immortals of Atlantis – Brian Stableford   Selected for 'Year's Best'
Terminal – Chaz Brenchley   Placed 3rd, best short story, BSFA Awards
Among Strangers – Pat Cadigan Selected for the Locus recommended
reading list
Cracked Earth (cover) **– Andy Bigwood** Winner best artwork BSFA Awards

**"Some of the best and most solidly science fiction-oriented anthologies
of the year were almost stealth-published. Best of these was
disLOCATIONS, edited by Ian Whates..." –** *Gardner Dozois.*

www.newconpress.com

THE BRITISH SCIENCE FICTION ASSOCIATION

Don't just *read* about British science fiction… be a part of it.

Proud of our history and excited by the future.

The British Science Fiction Association: over 50 years of providing a focus for the people who love to read, watch, learn about and talk about science fiction.

Why join the BSFA? Well…

1. **The Community of Fans**

2. **Exclusive Magazines**

3. **Exclusive Discounts on Books**

4. **Support and Advice for New Writers**

5. **The Very Best of Reviews and Informed Opinion**

6. **Keeping Up to Date With News and Events**

7. **The Ability to Vote in the BSFA Awards**

8. **Affordable Membership Fees**

WHY MISS OUT?

To discover more, visit our website and forums at
www.bsfa.co.uk/bsfa/website/default.aspx